I0738690

REAL COPS

BY THE SAME AUTHOR

BOOKS

The Gypsy Twist

Funny Bunny Hunts the Horn Bug

Brownstone Kidnap Crackup

Can Showbizzers Crush Crime?

Softening Flatbush

*When the Whistle Blows,
Everyone Goes*

*Max Wisecracks Hollywood or
Foxtrotting for Justice*

*Love Finds Max Royster or
Kissing in the Slush after Sixty*

*Dancing Max Hits Guadalcanal or
When In Doubt, Rhumba*

FEATURE FILMS

Spy, The Movie
(co-written with Charles Messina
& Lynwood Shiva Sawyer)

REAL COPS

by Frank Hickey

Brooklyn • London
Fincastle

Real Cops

Copyright © 2020 Frank Hickey

Book Design by D. Bass
Cover design by Jamie Bauermeister
Original cover painting by Nad Wolinksa (All rights reserved)

ISBN: 978-1-7331750-2-9
Library of Congress Control Number: 2020911826

Catalogue-in-Publication Data Real Cops / Frank Hickey
1. Fiction – Crime 2. Fiction – Mystery 3. Fiction – Historical

All rights reserved. No part of this book may be reproduced or utilized in any form or by any means, mechanical or electronic, including manual re-input, photocopying, scanning, optical character recognition, recording or by any information storage and retrieval system without permission in writing from the copyright holder.

For purposes of this narrative, the role played by certain historical figures such as J. Edgar Hoover, Melvin Purvis, Pretty Boy Floyd, John Dillinger, etc., and historical incidents such as the Kansas City Massacre, have been partially fictionalized. To the greatest degree possible, depictions of these characters and incidents abide by the generally accepted facts of biography and history. Other characters and incidents are the product of the author's imagination. Any resemblance of the non-historical figures and events to actual persons, living or dead, or actual events, is purely coincidental.

For further information, please contact:
http://frankhickey.net

Published by Pigtown Books

10 9 8 7 6 5 4 3 2 1
First Edition / First Issue
Pigtown Books Logo and Colophon designed by Richard Amari

Dedicated to all the women and men,
Special Agents and Support Staff of the
Federal Bureau of Investigation,
past and present.

PART I

PROLOGUE

CHAPTER 1: Wednesday, November 9, 1932

NORTH INDIANA

In the cold dawn after Election Day, Lee Childress was driving down miles of country roads. He was slightly built, with fair hair and deep blue eyes. His silver-framed eyeglasses made him look mild and lawyerly.

The voters had come in quickly yesterday and showed that Herbert Hoover was defeated, carrying only six states. The last gas pump jockey had told Lee that voters had picked Franklin Delano Roosevelt as their new president.

At last the sun rose, lighting up the bleak countryside and turning the new snow pink.

Lee drove the car past two big bay horses standing by the roadside, reins dragging.

Seeing their riders tramping through the high brush next to the road, covered with snow, Lee braked and backed up to the horses. He stopped the Ford on the road's shoulder.

The two horsemen had silver stars pinned to their coats and heavy gun belts around their waists. Lee scrambled out of the driver's seat, hugging the winter car coat around him.

"You're policemen?" Lee asked. "Can I help you?"

One of the men blocked Lee.

"Sheriff's officers," he said. "Keep going, partner. Y'all move that machine out, hear?"

Lee looked past them.

There was a dead body lying like a lump of rags along the hard ground. The legs were tucked in like the body was trying to stay warm.

Lee reached into his breast pocket and showed the black leather credentials folder with the tiny tin badge pinned to the back.

"I'm from the U.S. Department of Justice in Chicago," he said. "Name of Lee Childress. Can I help you here?"

"Prohibition man?"

"Nossir," Lee said. "Bureau of Investigation. I'm a po-lice, just like you."

The deputy snorted and examined Lee's credentials, a card encased in plastic. The credentials looked like a dollar bill with greenish scrollwork at the top. The lettering in the scrollwork read "United States Department of Justice."

The photograph on the card showed Lee with shorter hair and the look of a spanked schoolboy.

Lee's light, clear voice made the deputy turn his lips down in a sneer.

The older deputy showed broken front teeth and a dead white scar high on his cheek. Lee recognized the scar as a buckshot wound.

"I've got a thermos of hot coffee in the car," Lee said. "If you'd like to warm up some. I figure you must be frozen and might want to get off your feet for a while. Takes a tough man to patrol on horseback in winter."

"Youngster, we been up all night, waiting for our coroner. It was cold and it's going to stay cold. We don't need you or your coffee to do our job."

Lee shut up and looked back at the car, twelve feet away on the roadway. Birds cawed high overhead. Lee's mouth tasted of coffee. A wool smell from the dead body's clothes mixed with the scent of his own tweed topcoat. Cold knifed through him.

He could tell these old boys were riled and planning to push him around some.

That is why the Bureau should issue us bigger shiny gold badges, he thought. To get respect from Hoosier country coppers who never learned how to read credentials.

"You've got federal land all around here," Lee said. It was a guess. "And we're near the state line. That makes it a good bet that your dead body falls within my jurisdiction."

"Hellfire, you must be a lawyer," the younger deputy said. Carroty-colored hair crisped out from under his wool Stetson cowboy hat. "You sound just like a lawyer."

Lee's fair face flushed. His hands tightened into fists. The deputies snickered.

"Your dead man's probably some hood from Chicago," Lee said. "I've got a kit in the car and can fingerprint him right away."

"Nope," the older deputy smacked his gloved hands together, challenging Lee. "Whatever you can do is get out of here, Mister Government lawyer."

"You're worried about what I might find out?" Lee asked, stepping in closer.

"I don't think the Government's got nothing to do with po-licing," the deputy said. "You spy on one politician so you can tell another one about him. Then Congress pats you on the head and somebody loses an election."

He looked at the business suit and necktie Lee wore.

"You federal guys don't even look like real cops."

"We are," Lee said.

The younger deputy spat on the snow.

"You ain't nothing," the younger deputy said. "You heard my partner. Now get lost and stay there."

He shoved Lee back.

Lee slipped and fell in the snow, between the two of them.

He felt his face burning mad, the way it used to feel when he sparred against the bigger boys in college.

His feet twitched and started to walk away. But he locked his legs until the shaking stopped. Then he tossed his head and tried to look tough, like the coppers in the movies.

"Deputy, maybe you and me better have a little talk," Lee said. His voice cracked. Both deputies smirked. "Just you and me. You man enough?"

"Well, you're real entertaining, kid," the younger one said.

He was silent as Lee pocketed his own eyeglasses.

The wind picked up. The smell of leather horse tack drifted to them. Lee walked a few yards from the dead man and dropped his car coat in the snow.

He spoke with a soft Midwestern twang. But his hands showed scars and nicks from farm work and college boxing.

The younger deputy was big through the shoulders and gut, with a flat face that somebody had kicked around. He handed his leather uniform coat, silver star flashing, to his partner who stood smirking.

The deputy stepped in first. He threw a hook punch. Lee weaved and put a tight right hand into the bigger man's belly. It sank in and Lee jabbed him twice. The deputy shook, then swung a left that stung Lee's cheek.

Lee faked and jabbed again.

The deputy took it, then hit another right hand to Lee's mouth, bloodying it. A fist banged his eye.

Lee swayed. His left snapped into the grizzled face. He threw a right cross and moved in to finish. But the deputy stayed up.

He hit Lee on the heart and then whipped out three more punches to the body. Lee's wind went out. He covered up, hunching over. The deputy slammed his face with a hook and then moved around, both hands battering Lee's face.

Lee staggered. The deputy threw more punches, moved back and let Lee fall full length in the snow.

Lee rolled and curled up, blood flowing onto his Pierce-Arrow collar, snow slipping down his back. He blinked his eyes, like a baby waking up.

The deputy slapped his partner on the arm.

"Everything's jake," the deputy said. "You done fine."

He looked down at Lee.

"The way I see it, youngster, we just won the state of Indiana back from the U.S. Government."

That got Lee up onto his feet. Lee shook.

"I didn't say that I was through, Bubba," Lee said.

"You don't have to," the deputy said. "Your face did. Now you drive on outta here and don't come back. You got any business in this county, forget it. We don't hold with your politics, not letting folks drink a li'l beer of a Sunday."

The fighting deputy nodded.

"Git," was all he said.

"You got no right to do this," Lee said. "We're the Justice. And we're sworn to investigate –"

"Where's your handgun, youngster?" the older deputy said. "You planning to investigate some hooligan without it? You kids can't arrest nobody without a real cop holding your hand."

"That's going to change," Lee said.

"Try arresting a killer with no pistol, and you'll see some changes right away."

"Loud ones," his partner said.

"The whole country laughs at you," the deputy said.

"Starting with us."

"You don't look like you shave yet," the partner said. "Never got no hank with your pants off. Dressed up like a banker in that suit and necktie."

"Regulations," Lee said. "Business attire at all times."

"You're here because of our fool Congressman," the partner said. "The married one."

"With the redhead mistress who pleasures everyone," the deputy said. "And all their forged Government checks. That's no secret. My wife is tongue-wagging about it all day. So do her friends. Newspapers print it."

Lee gulped and jerked his head up to stare at them.

"You can't know why I'm here," Lee said. His voice wavered in the wind.

"Tell me another one. Our sheriff says that you federals will sneak around here and dig up dirt against the Republicans and hurt them in the next election."

"I hear that you kids are all lawyers and accountants," the older one said. "Did you go through law school for that?"

Lee bent down, picked up his car coat and began to weave his way back to the Bureau car. Losing the fight gritted his teeth.

"Tell me that we're wrong," the younger deputy said. "Go ahead and lie for your bosses."

"You're right," Lee said under his breath. "Everything that you said. That just makes it worse."

CHAPTER 2: November 1932

PRAGUE, OKLAHOMA

Pretty Boy Floyd was sleeping next to a teenage Osage Indian whore in the Oklahoma woods. He woke before her, watching the morning sunlight dapple the twists of muscle along her spine. A plume of black hair covered her bony shoulders. Floyd put his canvas mackinaw over her so she would not catch cold.

"What happened?" she said, eyes closed. "You want something special? Maybe the gypsy twist?"

Her hard little hands brushed him.

"Want to see you sleep," he whispered. "That's special enough."

"What happened?"

She always asked that question. It made him grin.

She curled up again, like a kid.

"You wouldn't get it, anyway," he whispered. "But a man running needs to hole up with a bottle or a woman sometimes to get some peace."

Floyd's voice dipped and rolled like the hills around him. His twang sounded like he talked through his nose.

"What happened?"

Her voice burred. She probably spoke more Osage Indian than English.

He heard the birds hit their morning song. They threw chips of sound through the woods.

Floyd scanned the woods, looking for any sign of the law-dogs. This hidey-hole held the high ground. Nobody could sneak up on him. Thirty feet away, the Hudson was half-hidden in the brush.

His gang still snored and belched in the seats. Floyd swung to his feet and walked behind a grove of saplings to ease himself. A leafy smell tickled his nose.

He was a beefy man with a baby face turning mean and a mouth ready to cuss. Enemies said that he looked like a weak king losing control.

Hair furred his body. Thick eyebrows echoed the chest hair. His jowls turned blue with stubble. Hair scored the backs of his fingers. Birds twitted, making his blue-gray eyes hopscotch through the saplings. Gunslinger's eyes, everyone said.

Choosing hidey-holes like this one had kept him alive so far. He tapped the Colt Government Model in his belt as he stretched, making sure the .45 clip was seated by the walnut grips.

His back muscles clicked, stiff from the last four nights, jammed into the rumble seat.

He made sure that his gang still slept and then he moved back to the sleeping whore. He fingered her secret skin.

She moved and wetted.

"Now I'll show you what happened," he breathed.

Afterwards, he lay on his back, just floating with the feel of her. His nerves buttered.

"You bring me here, to dream-land," he whispered.

She giggled and curled up against him.

They slept some more. Sunlight tightened around them.

"You use me like an animal," she said. "But I don't mind."

"Here, take this cash," he said. "The extra is for what you did. And for walking back. We can't give no ride back to the roadhouse."

"Okay," she said. "I'll hitchhike back. Everyone knows me. I'm sorry that you miss your wife and little boy so much."

"Me, too."

Then she was up and walking back down the road. Floyd closed his eyes.

The morning sounds were changing. Birds slowed their songs. He felt the cords of his own body tying up for the day to come.

"Like to keep her longer," he muttered. "Time to move now."

Floyd stepped to the car and poked his head through the window. Sweat smell met him.

"You boys figure to sleep all day?" he asked.

Birdwell and C.C. Patterson sat up inside the car, unbuttoning the coats they had slept in. A dried-out, string bean Okie, George Birdwell, dressed in overalls, hairy wool shirt and black brogan boots.

To Floyd's eye, Patterson belonged on the farm, not robbing banks. If men were animals, Patterson would make a good plough mule, sullen and blocky and needing a whipping sometimes. His faded farm clothes still held some dry mud.

"Where's the hooker?" Patterson asked. "She's cute. I wanted a squirrel shot myself."

Floyd chilled his own eyes and gunned Patterson with them. He spat on the ground, fronting off these losers.

Patterson sucked on a broken front tooth and looked away.

Floyd kept staring at Patterson.

"Why are we freezing up here?" Birdwell asked.

"Because Oklahoma is hot for us after that last job in Atoka," Floyd said. "So we riding the cat roads. So narrow and rough that only a cat can run them. No law-dogs ride them."

Johnny Glass rolled over on his Navajo blanket spread across the ground. His black skin shone. Like a lot of Oklahomans, he was part Osage. That blood showed in his wide moon face and thick chest tapering to narrow legs.

"I could use some coffee," Glass said, creaking up to his feet. "For a good warming up."

"Just be glad it didn't rain," Pretty Boy Floyd told him sourly. Glass turned Floyd's mouth tighter. "Don't try to sleep in a car with White folks."

"That's right," Birdwell said. "You're on this job just so you can blend into Boley and your color is your meal ticket on this job, Glassy. Don't push it."

Birdwell took a sawed-off pump shotgun and two .45s from the floor. Chunky yellow ammo boxes littered the seat.

"I'm curious about this town, Boley. I never seen a town that was all Nee-gro, wall to wall." Floyd lifted out his Thompson gun. The gun showed three feet of blued steel and wood stock and grips. Gun oil slicked the metal.

Floyd unsnapped the wooden stock and examined the receiver. His fingers probed and explored. Catches snicked into place. He hefted the fat round magazine with 50 slugs fit next to the trigger. The wood grips shone in the sunlight like fine furniture. The others watched his skill.

"That right about Boley, Glassy?" Floyd asked.

"That's right. Nothing but colored folks in Boley. Mayor, judge and everyone else. Runaway slaves built the town before the Civil War. They used to shoot at any White man that came near and there are still no Whites living there. And now, they're doing well by themselves, living better than most towns these days."

"I don't know, Floyd," Patterson said. "I've been tipped by friends that the bank isn't as helpless as it looks. We could get ourselves killed if we aren't careful. Coloreds is bad luck."

"And so is cowards," Floyd said. "Colored money spends green and sweet, just like white. So let's stop the jawing and get to it."

CHAPTER 3: November 9 1932

BOLEY, OKLAHOMA

Close to town in the Hudson, Birdwell crossed a truck's ignition wires and started the truck up.

Floyd crawled into the back with his Thompson and four ammo drums and writhed himself under the hay. He was the "keep away man."

If any fool tried to stop the bank job, Floyd would cut them down with the Tommy. He could put out 600 rounds per minute, hitting everything within 50 yards. He felt the hay poke his belly as he scanned the town.

Floyd waited until Birdwell left. Then he put two smoke-bombs in their fat gray Army cases next to him. His thumb toyed with the switches.

Glass chewed on his lips from nerves.

Inside the Farmers Bank, H.C. McCormick, the bookkeeper passed between the vault and the one teller's cage, carrying the statements file.

"Why you rushing so?" Hiram asked.

"We should wind up the morning count quick," McCormick said. "Governor Murray kicking off the bird season today, right after Election Day."

"We sure love our hunting in Boley. The only way to sling meat on the table in these hard times. Eufal's hardware store was having a sale, rifles and shotguns. I need to get there before all the specials sell out."

Cyrus Turner, the bank president, sat behind his roll-top desk, scanning the mail and the morning's Tulsa World. Hiram was in the teller's cage, cupping a rolled-up Bull Durham cigarette in his big farm worker's hands.

"When is Mr. Turner leaving?" Hiram whispered. "I crave a smoke real bad, but he'll give me hell for puffing up smoking in the teller's cage."

"Give him a minute," McCormick said. "Something will happen."

Looking over the side of the truck, Floyd could see that the streets of Boley were filled with Black citizens. Nobody seemed to be carrying guns. It was different from Sallisaw, Floyd's home town, where they toted hunting rifles everywhere. Floyd grinned to see Boley as a soft touch.

Floyd looked across the town square at some cornfields. If they had to make a break, they could run there. From his other jobs, Floyd knew that a cornfield was a good place to hide and get away from the law-dogs.

Two brass Civil War cannon lay on the town square. Behind them, an alley ran alongside a red-brick schoolhouse. Floyd opened and shut his eyes. He memorized how far the cannon lay from his truck and the alley.

Floyd smiled again. Now he could run it blindfolded. He torched up a Newman cigar and puffed.

Birdwell and Patterson saw Glass outside the bank and they parked the Hudson at the curb. They wore big hats to hide their white faces. Glass went inside the bank first and scanned it. Glass came out and nodded to them.

Birdwell and Patterson entered together.

Birdwell walked up to Turner's desk and shoved a nickel-plated .45 against the president's breastbone. Turner went slack. He saw two other men, one Black, were already flanking Hiram, their own .45's close to his frightened face.

"It's a stick-up, boys," Patterson shouted. "First one blinks is gonna wake up dead."

Nobody had seen McCormick since he was inside the vault, with his statements file. He was caught there, with nowhere to run. His hands shook.

He stooped down slowly and his hand felt for an old Winchester they kept there in case of robbery, watching Birdwell while he moved.

"Get them bunched," he whispered. "Like ducks."

Glass reached into Hiram's drawer and yanked out all the bills. Two alarm electrodes came together but made no noise in the bank. Glass had no idea that the alarm rang in the sheriff's office and both hardware stores. The stores were full of customers buying guns and ammo. When the bell rang, the clerks passed out free samples.

McCormick picked up his Winchester, still inside the vault.

He was just a dozen feet from where the robbers stood. No one had seen him. He sighted on Birdwell's heart region, held his breath and fired. The bullet spun Birdwell around. He went down, reaching for Turner.

"You!" he rasped out. "You help me up, Mister Darkey! Give me a hand–". Turner stooped and grabbed him under the arms. A vest button snapped. Birdwell rose and shoved his pistol into the vest, triggering it. Turner screamed. Birdwell kept firing, face pale under the stubble. The slugs pushed Turner against the roll-top desk and then the floor. He lay still.

Glass's nerve broke when Turner fell. He ran yelping to the bank's front door. Shotguns blasted him back. The street was full of Black farmers, pumping rounds into the bank. Glass was dead before he started to fall, the first good clean hit of the bird season.

Patterson had been trading shots with McCormick. The book-keeper put two slugs past Patterson's ear, panicking him. Patterson leaped over Birdwell and out the front door.

The hunters outside never stopped firing. Patterson's faded work shirt turned red instantly, spurting blood.

The farmers kept firing.

"This is a lynching the right way for once," one said. "Mess with our bank? Keep shooting these crackers all day."

Lying on his belly in the farm truck, Floyd saw everything. He ripped off the smoke-bomb switches and tossed them in front of the truck. He crawled up into the driver's seat. He tried to re-cross the wires and start the engine again. But someone saw his white face and started shooting. Then the smoke covered everything.

"What's afire?" a small Black man said.

"Nobody knows."

The engine caught.

"Can't see anything."

The smoke covered a knot of locals. They gagged and choked.

"You won't shoot what you can't see," Floyd grinned.

Floyd coughed but fired a Tommy gun burst across the street. Nobody could see anything.

Floyd lit the straw with his cigar.

Orange flame ran along the straw. He tossed an ammo drum on the fire.

Floyd slid out of the truck. His hands still held the Tommy. Counting steps, he ran to the Civil War cannons and squatted down. The smoke hid him.

Bullets cracked. He recognized the sound of .45 slugs. The ammo drum inside the truck was afire now, the heat exploding the bullets. Farmers screamed and dropped. Floyd heard the bullets hit TANG! on the cannons near him. He knew the cast-iron metal of the cannons would protect him. He had planned it this way.

More bullets whined from the truck.

The truck exploded. Floyd smelled gas from the shot tank.

Pieces of something rained through the air.

"Now!" Floyd said.

He counted eight steps from the cannons to the school-house. He passed his hand on the wall until he felt the corner and the lane alongside it.

Floyd ran down the lane. He left the smoke behind him.

The lane came out onto another street. It was just like he had planned.

A white-haired Black farmer in overalls was standing by his truck. His hands gripped an old Winchester lever-action 30-30. He gaped at Floyd's Tommy gun snout.

"You're too slow, Senior," Floyd said. "Raise them."

The grandpappy hesitated.

Floyd ripped a burst at his feet.

The Winchester dropped.

"Need to borrow that vehicle," Floyd said. "You'll get it back."

Farmers hollered and shot at Floyd. One slug hit the Grandpappy in the back patch pocket of his overalls. He dropped, cussing words that Floyd had never heard before.

Floyd gunned the engine and wove the truck down the street, making it a tougher target to hit. Bullets snapped into the truck, but Floyd was going fast now, humping his way out of Boley.

"Keep shooting," he said. "My luck still holds. Nobody stops Pretty Boy Floyd."

PART II

STARTING FROM SCRATCH

CHAPTER 4: June 1932

Lee had grown up on a farm outside of Omaha, Nebraska. His father had wanted all the boys to be professional men, not tied to crops and harvesting. Lee suffered through college, almost flunking out twice, and clerked for a lawyer in his spare time. He wanted to try lawyering himself. Two years of college allowed Lee to enter Creighton University School of Law.

But in the Depression, not many wanted to try it. Judges got by on bread and gravy for lunch. Lawyers seemed a luxury that people could do without until things got straightened out.

When the stock market had crashed in '29, nobody in Omaha gave it much thought at first. Wall Street was like Belleau Wood had been, a million miles away.

By the spring of 1932, everyone knew better, and the country was struggling to stay alive. Gossips hissed that Omaha would be crippled for a long time. Lee's boss, Will Keithly, had watched his own law practice dry up. He was a fattish young father with heavy glasses and thinning, pale hair, parted in the middle. Will always wore somber dark suits and ties, trying to show how serious practicing law should be.

During Lee's final year in law school, he and Lee got into the habit of discussing law while they drank bootleg rye late into

Saturday night. They would spend hours in front of the fireplace discussing constitutional action.

They talked about law the way other men talked about baseball or women.

They both knew the states needed federal help to survive. But local government had always rebelled against interference from Washington. From the Revolutionary War, through the Civil War and right to the present, nothing had changed. Government was still a local affair and Washington, D.C. had never stepped in to help the working man.

There was not enough business for two lawyers in Will Keithly's office. So Lee could not keep his law clerk's job once he passed the bar examination. He trudged through around Omaha and heard the bitter Depression wisecracks.

One old friend would come into his pal's dying business and point a finger, saying, "This is a stickup."

Then they would fall over each other laughing. But there was nothing funny about it.

The Army was not accepting officers. They were not taking privates at $20 a month, either.

"The idea of going into the military after my law schooling sets my teeth on edge," Lee told Will.

"It will give you a roof over your head and grubs," Will said. "Like the hoboes say, three hots and a cot. You do not want to hang around the downtown area and wait for things to get better. Anyone who does that is a chump."

On the last Friday in June, Lee spent all day trying to find a job with the federal government. He walked into the Omaha Post Office building at lunchtime. He had never thought much of the Washington government. Neither did anyone else in Omaha.

The federal bureaus were just a row of poky little offices, each one with a receptionist next to a picture of Herbert Hoover and the American flag. Soap mixed with cigar smell.

"Help you?" the receptionist asked.

"I didn't know there was this many government desks," Lee said. "I'm a quiet respectful feller who wants to work at anything honest. Somebody will throw me some kind of bone."

There was a sign taped to the U.S. Navy recruiting office:

DUE TO REDUCTIONS-IN-FORCE,
THE DEPARTMENT OF THE
NAVY IS NOT ACCEPTING NEW
APPLICATIONS AT THIS TIME.

Lee went back to the receptionist and asked which offices were open. A radio played banjo music. Nerves rosed his cheeks.

"Well, that depends," she said, pushing pince-nez glasses. "What's your trade?"

"Lawyer," he answered, feeling the scratchy shirt-collar pinch.

"Well, you just go down the hall to the Department of Justice. See Mr. Price there. Sign says 'Justice,' so they must need lawyers for something."

"For something," Lee agreed.

He walked along the wooden plank flooring. A bronze plaque on the door said "Department of Justice, United States of America."

A fat man with pop eyes was seated comfortably behind a roll-top desk. He wore half-moon glasses on his wide face and his thick-gray hair was brushed back.

He looked like one of the Katzenjammer kids in the funnies. A cigar the size of a bread stick lolled in his fat hand.

"What can I do for you, son?" he asked, looking Lee over.

"My name is Lee Childress." His voice climbed and shook. "I'm a lawyer and interested in a job with the Justice Department."

"Being a lawyer right now means nothing," the fat man said, rolling the cigar in his soft hand. "Lots of lawyers are out there looking for work, son. What have you got that would make Uncle Sam want to hire you? "

The room would excite no one. A window looked out over the Post Office truck loading docks and the gray curtains hung limp along the windowsill. There was an American flag mounted on a stand next to the window.

Over the fat man's desk there was a colored seal of a winged eagle marked JUSTICE. Lee thought the eagle looked angry about something.

"Well, if you sit down, you might learn something." The fat man did not sound hopeful. "Now, I work for an outfit that Congress keeps hog-tied and broke. You ever heard of the Bureau of Investigation? We dig up information for one politician so he can sling mud at another politician."

This sounded like plain talk,

"Is it dirty work?" Lee asked.

"Do fat babies fart? " the man asked.

Lee considered this.

"We got this young Director named Hoover," the fat man wheezed. "No relation to the President Hoover. Our Director is trying to push us into criminal jurisdiction, but it won't work. The people have enough cops and Prohibition men telling them what to do already. So they won't want us acting like cops. We'll still be the same two-bit silly outfit we were when I joined up in '08 but there is one thing we do very well."

"What's that?"

"What we're told. We do that real well. If the Director wants us to stay out of sight, we stay out of sight. We work real quiet and don't go near the firing line.

"Let these hillbillies kill each other off.

"Now you're a lawyer. You know that Uncle Sam can't inter-fere with the states' doings. If we did, we'd be acting illegally. Had a little fracas called the Civil War over that question a while back. Now, we're not policemen. Get that through your head if you want to apply. We're a fact-finding agency that obeys whatever nincompoop is in the White House. It's a very political job but it's easy work."

The man tapped a blue binder with his cigar.

"We make our recommendations on land fraud cases, anti-trust cases, the bucket-shop laws, the Mann Act relating to interstate commerce, laws relating to fraudulent bankruptcy and the Dyer Act on driving stolen cars across state lines. How's that sound?"

He grinned at Lee, with regular white teeth, store-bought choppers.

"Dry, legal, technical and safe. I'd like to apply."

"Whoa. Let me tell you the facts of life here. Might be you're gonna to have to know someone to get a job. Otherwise, you're wasting your time. There are going to be openings in other agencies for lawyers. I think you should hold out for them."

Lee shook his head.

"If you have application forms," Lee said, "I'd like to get started on them now."

"The pay stinks. Everyone laughs at us. You really want to apply?"

Lee thought of steady Government paychecks and hot meals and he nodded his blond head. "You betcha I do. A fella turning down a chance right now would have to be a real chump."

CHAPTER 5: Tuesday, September 12, 1932

OMAHA, NEBRASKA

The corn stalks were turning brown in the Childress fields before Lee heard anything.

Shorty, the boy from the telegraph office, bicycled out to deliver a telegram. The yellow script offered probationary appointment as a Special Agent at $2,900 per year. None of Lee's family had ever heard of the Bureau of Investigation. Neither had Shorty.

Everyone looked at the telegram and handed it around the family like it was something magic from an enchanted land.

"I'm fixing a cautious celebration dinner of country ham, baked potatoes, succotash and chocolate cake," Lee's mom said. Lee got his pale face and fair hair from her, along with weak eyes behind her rimless glasses. Lee was always worried that her glasses would break.

"Why a cautious celebration?" Lee asked.

"Cautious cause you don't know what you're getting into. None of us do. And it scares me pink."

"If I stay here," Lee said, "I'll feel like I never grew up. Just hiding out inside the family."

Lee and Pop went for a walk across the fields after dinner. It was a warm night with a dry wind blowing long gusts across the farm. The stars hung close and bright.

"Lee, gangsters are taking over, with their bulletproof cars that outrun the cops. Good girls turned gun molls love and protect these hooligans. These Government men can't find who kidnapped the Lindbergh baby. Got ransom kidnappings everywhere."

"Have you bought an apple from a banker recently?" Lee asked. "You must have heard about schoolteachers fainting from hunger while they're teaching a class? Don't worry about me. I'll work clean."

"You're a lawyer," Pop muttered. "I don't see why you're going to take this kind of job."

"It's a job where I use the law. I'll starve as a new lawyer in town."

"You know there's never been a police group that decent people respected."

Pop was a reader who spoke his own mind.

"Never," he said. "Nobody trusts their honesty. Payoffs, easy money, bosses who don't work. Your local politician puts your name up for the police to hire you. Then you dance to their tune. There's never been a police force that I wanted you or your brothers to have anything to do with. Go on, now, tell me I'm wrong."

"This is a new kind of police."

"Lee, you always believe everyone."

"C'mon, Pop. This isn't really policing. It's investigating. That's different."

"Really different," Pop snorted. "You'll be investigating Senators. Checking one politician and telling another. Taking poor people's nickels and locking them up when the boss tells you to."

"I need to work at something."

"This is the wrong way to put bread on the table. The country'll snap out of this fix soon."

"How's the country doing lately? Don't worry about me. I'll work clean."

"That's what you think. Politics. Standard Oil. Teapot Dome." He kicked some of his own earth. "You'll see. If you want to work clean, they won't let you do much."

CHAPTER 6: Late September 1932

WASHINGTON, D.C.

Lee entered a huge, high-ceilinged courtroom with dark brown wooden benches. Neat stacks of books and manuals lay on the top of each stack, alongside a black leather folding wallet.

Fourteen clean-cut college boys, the new agents class of 1932, clustered together, uncertain of what would happen next. Sunlight streamed in through stained-glass windows. Portraits of Washington and Lincoln hung on the walls. It reminded Lee of a castle showing the majesty of the law.

He had met some of his workmates on the sleeper train he took from Omaha. Some had been wearing raccoon coats and college scarves. Now all were dressed in suits and ties. Some of the suits fit badly. They were mail-order suits, sent to farms.

Lee heard different accents for the first time.

"You from Scotland?" he asked fresh-faced redhead with freckles. "You talk different."

"Rhode Island."

"Hey, everybody," a reedy clerk-type next to Lee whispered. "What is a 'Special Agent'? And what is he supposed to do?"

Lee shrugged.

"You youngsters settle down," a slim older clerk snapped in a Southern drawl. "Knock off the hoo-raw-raw and line up in formation!"

The clerk had plastered-down snowy-gray hair, with his nose like a dagger dividing his face.

"Why?" a new agent asked. He showed a broad dark face over his tight buttoned collar. To Lee, he looked like one of the Indians hanging around downtown Omaha. "We're not military. Just fact-finders. Nothin' silly like saluting."

"Because, gentlemen," the clerk said, his thin face twisting. "I'm Chief Clerk John Martiska and this is my territory."

Like children, the new agents hushed and lined up.

"Some of you heroes may be going undercover," Martiska continued. "So the public's not allowed in here. Now. Please raise your right hands and repeat after me. 'I, insert name, do solemnly swear –"

The new agents repeated the phrase with their names.

Martiska continued. He paused at some places to allow the new agents to repeat his words.

"'That I will support and defend the Constitution of the United States against all enemies, foreign and domestic; that I will bear true faith and allegiance to the same; that I take this obligation freely, without any mental reservation or purpose of evasion; and that I will well and faithfully discharge the duties of the office on which I am about to enter. So help me God.'"

Lee was standing on the end at the left of the line.

"Name?"

"Lee Childress."

Martiska shook his hand.

"Congratulations."

He thumbed through a stack of ID cards and handed it to Lee.

"It's got your name and it's been signed by the Director and the Attorney General."

A foreign-looking, well-dressed man swept in. His blue alpaca suit was finer and better cut than any of theirs. Eyes squinted under black brows.

Martiska stiffened to attention, "Gentlemen, meet your Director, J. Edgar Hoover."

Twelve years older than Lee, Hoover had been a young lawyer himself not too long ago.

Hoover addressed the new recruits with quiet intensity, his dark eyes flashing. In a voice that was a flat, dry rattle he spoke of new goals to strive for, the dawn of powerful federal intervention. The Bureau of Investigation would be a new agency where procedure counted for more than personality. He wanted each field office and each agent to operate in the same way. This would be the first police agency in the world where citizens would have complete confidence in the policemen.

When Hoover left, Martiska led them over to the bench with the stacks of books. He palmed a black leather wallet from the first stack and flipped it open to reveal an ugly gold badge, insultingly small. It looked like a fat gob of butter, topped by that same angry eagle of justice.

"After we've stuck your photo onto your ID card, you will place it in this wallet. These are your credentials. Whenever you bravos interview a citizen, ya must show the credentials and give your name."

"What about when we arrest somebody?" the reedy new agent asked.

"Cripes sakes, you pups ain't gonna arrest nobody," said Martiska, "You're not even allowed to carry weapons, without special permission."

He handed the wallet to Lee, "Use your credentials to get train tickets – on official business, only. Keep your creds with you at all times."

He then handed the manual of rules, federal law books, and government travel pads

After he had handed out the wallets and books, Martiska talked the agents into another room for their ID pictures.

CHAPTER 7: October 1932

CHICAGO, ILLINOIS

The new agents underwent two weeks of training and indoctrination. Their teachers warned them repeatedly that they could not carry any kind of gun without approval. They could not make arrests without the police at their elbows.

After the final lecture, the agents were split up and sent to different offices throughout the country.

Lee was assigned to the Chicago Field Office under the direction of a Special Agent in Charge named Melvin Purvis.

Lee's first day was on a chilly autumn day with the wind howling.

He woke in his rented room, dressed and took the streetcar to Clark and Adams, near the United States Courthouse. Feeling like a little kid on his first day of school, he walked to the Bankers Building where the Bureau of Investigation had its offices on the nineteenth floor.

Lee showed his letter of introduction to the file clerk, a thin, darkish man with graying hair and a hard-looking pot belly. The clerk wore a stained yellow shirt with a pop-'em bowtie and a pair of greasy green slacks.

"Let me tell you something, my friend," the file clerk said. "You're brand-new in the Bureau so I'll let you in on an old saying. Clerks run the Bureau. We know people, we listen at doors, we've been here longer and we make more money than you agents. Keep that in mind.

"Now, anytime you leave the office, you fill out a Number Three card. One of these. You list where you're gonna be, who you're gonna see, and for how long. Don't ever try to fudge these. We check you. And the boss checks us. And the inspectors check the boss. Got it?

"We are not the police or the military here. We don't salute or sport uniforms. But you must wear a clean suit and white shirt every darn day. Nobody cares how you manage that. Do it. Our rank names are the same as the railroad company ranks. It goes, special agent, supervisory special agent, supervisor, general cases supervisor, assistant special agent in charge and special agent in charge."

"Why do we copy the railroad?" Lee asked. "Are we running a railroad?"

"Sometimes I can't figure just what we are running. We do that so that we don't scare the taxpayers with new ranks. These titles have been broken in. Everyone likes and trusts the railroad. They let conductors watch their brats."

"It sounds like we're trying to fool people."

"We are. Anything you learn in an interview goes on an FD Form 302. One of these. Anything at all.

"You handwrite your own reports and they better be neat. Don't ever go to a dame's house without another agent. If she screams rape, you've got a witness.

"Don't try to pick up dames while you're working or you'll get canned. You whistle at some dame in the Loop, she's liable to be the Mayor's girlfriend.

"When a case comes in, you record it on a complaint form. The group supervisor then decides who tries to work it. We say that the agent 'has the ticket' on the case. If he fouls up, he gets burnt. The agent who has the ticket runs the indices. These are our files. The indices give him the info on the victim, the location, or the subject. We call the bad guy the subject here. Get used to it. The file clerk then opens a file on the new case and gives it a serial number. The case is kept on the rotary file in your area. Everything dealing with the case is kept in your work box. Guess what happens if you lose anything."

"Listen, sir, I can't take all this in."

"Canned. They're all charged to you. Your responsibility."

The clerk's eyes glowed, briefly, like the stubby Picayune he was smoking.

"Every night, you gosh-darn well better lock your work box in the safe. If you ever get lucky enough to close a case, the file clerk takes the files from you and puts them in the permanent se-rial files in the office. Another file gets sent to Bureau headquarters in Washington. They go over it real careful there. Oh, yeah. With a fine-tooth comb. You phony something up, and they'll know, believe me, they'll know. But you won't get out of the office for six months, since you're new."

Lee wondered how he could listen to six months of the chief clerk's talk while other agents were out on the street solving mys-terious cases and fighting crime.

He wanted to work hard at his first real job and not just collect a paycheck. The clerk sounded like all the other tired civil servants Lee had ever known.

The field office itself was comfortable and reminded him of a men's club with mahogany paneled walls and saddle-broke leather armchairs. It was for members only, with secret deals done in whispers.

"This room is the bull-pen." The clerk opened a door and pointed. About twenty desks and chairs jammed near each other.

"If you want to sleep while you're working, just make sure the door is shut tight. The boss, Mr. Purvis, he don't come in here. Whatever goes on in here, he don't want to know."

There was a hulk of a man sitting inside the bullpen with his feet up on a chair. He had pure white hair combed back from a huge craggy face. Lee figured him for about 60 years old, maybe an ex-heavyweight boxer gone to fat.

"Mr. Childress, this is Special Agent Brendan McQueeny. Childress here is from the new agents class," the clerk said. "Assigned to you, McQueeny. That means you're responsible."

"We don't need more kids," McQueeny said. "Youngster, if you work here, you'll be miserable. Help yourself. Resign now."

McQueeny burped.

"Okay," the clerk said. "Be a wiseguy. You're responsible for this new man here. Remember to fill out your Number Three cards if you go out."

"You fill 'em out," McQueeny growled. "Like always. You damn sure got my handwriting down pat. Who the hell are you trying to impress?"

The file clerk left and McQueeny looked Lee over.

"You a lawyer?" McQueeny asked.

Lee nodded.

"You a little confused about what we actually do?"

Lee kept nodding.

"You're not the only one," McQueeny sounded like a city boy from somewhere tough. "Resign. Please. This place is a goat rodeo. Think it over. But, if you stay, just remember when you got some cheap politician by the short hairs and he starts whining and singing the blues, it's a misunderstanding, a mistake, he's innocent. You just tell him," he paused, "you don't wanna know. Got that? You don't wanna know."

"I don't wanna know."

"'We don't wanna know'. It's the Federal service motto. In this job, every day pays the same and they all count towards 20. In 20 years, you retire."

He put on an Irish tweed cap, jamming it down over his sheepdog's head.

"In the meantime, you drive us normal jokers nuts. You got a place to live?"

"I need to find some place better. I just got in here yesterday."

"I know a real cheap and clean hotel for you on 27th Street and Wabash. But you won't stay here and you won't like the job. It's all politics. Let's go out and see Chicago, lawyer. Everything's for sale here. I'll show you this lousy, crooked town."

Chapter 8: Wednesday, November 9, 1932
Later That Day

CHICAGO, ILLINOIS

As Lee pulled the car through the downtown Loop traffic, he felt his battered face and tried to move his jaw without wincing. He wanted to drive home and lie down for about three days and nights but he could not do it. Bureau regulations ordered all agents to make a written report at the field office as soon as possible. He parked the Ford in the basement garage of the Bankers Building and took the elevator up to the 19th floor.

McQueeny was at his desk filling out a Sick Leave form. He winked at Lee. He ignored Lee's bruises. He did not want to know.

A chunky redheaded man, wearing a rain-softened tan Stetson, looked up as Lee limped into the bullpen. He was Lee's regular partner with years of wind, sun and whiskey showing his age. Bureau credentials listed him. as "H.T. Ross" but somehow he was nicknamed "Honey."

"Lee?" he asked. "What in the name of Texas happened to you?"

Lee told him.

The redhead Honey moved in for a closer inspection.

Honey had been a Texas Ranger for years before joining the Bureau. He wore the Stetson everywhere.

Honey had huge workman's hands, knotted with scars and flattened knuckles from oil-field work. He touched Lee's jaw with a finger tip.

"That hurt?" Honey asked.

"No," Lee lied. "None of it hurts, Honey. It just looks bad."

"Yeah. Tell me another one. The boss man, Melvin Purvis, is going to love to read this report. He'll want to have something on his desk as soon as he sees your mug. Have you told anyone else about this?"

"Nobody."

"Well, you're not going to. Purvis would keep you off the street filing papers for months if he knew the truth. You tell him you slipped and fell off the road while checking a flat tire. You hit your face on some rocks. That's how you got all bruised up."

"That's the stupidest story I've heard cooked up," Lee commented.

"Damn sure is. You and me and Purvis know that. But it lets him off the hook. You can't tell Purvis that when the country is falling apart from the Depression, you start fights. You don't even know where you are."

Honey's face was getting redder.

"This is a bureaucracy and you got to lie to survive in it. Nobody wants to hear the truth. Purvis sure don't."

"'We don't wanna know'" Lee quoted.

"That's right. We really don't."

"Is all this play-acting really worth it?"

"Yes, it is." Honey softened. "Bureau's got some of the best cops in the country now and we're gonna hit these dime-store bandits hard. Things are better off because we're here."

"It's ridiculous that we got to lie in order to do our job."

"That's as plain as the dick on a moose. And you'd better get used to it because it's not going to change," Honey said. "Come on with me. You're gonna have a family meal with us tonight."

•

Honey lived in a ramshackle railroad flat house on the South Side's Stony Island Avenue.

He was like a wild overgrown kid, competing with his own brood for mischief. He drank bootleg "bust-head" outdoors, in all kinds of weather. Honey highly recommended the treatment for young lawyers who found themselves growing pale.

His house was furnished with chairs and tables "borrowed" from different government offices. All the ashtrays showed the federal eagle on them. A large gilt U.S. DEPARTMENT OF JUSTICE plaque hung over his fireplace.

Honey noticed Lee's eyes drift to the plaque.

"Department of Justice?" Honey giggled, "There ain't no justice. You come into the field office looking for justice and that's what you'll find – 'just us'."

Honey's three kids rolled around the living room in a cloud of chaos. They paid no attention to their father nor the stranger with him.

A scrawny Texas mutt raced in and started barking.

"Santa Anna! Santa Anna!" the kids screeched.

The dog wore a leather collar marked PROPERTY OF THE U.S. CUSTOMS SERVICE – DO NOT REMOVE.

Santa Anna ran around in a circle as the children, whooping and hollering, pursued him.

The living room echoed like a playground run by the Katzenjammer Kids.

Honey's wife, Jan, emerged from the kitchen. She looked like a pioneer woman, able to clear timber and feed livestock. She wore her brown hair in bangs over a round tanned face.

Honey kissed her on the cheek, "Evening, Ranger Captain."

Jan broke away, freezing when she saw Lee's battered and bruised face,

"Jeepers creepers, Honey. Who is this skinny kid?"

Honey and Lee exchanged looks.

"I fell down the steps at my boarding house. I'm his new partner, Lee Childress."

"Purvis took Lee away from McQueeny and gave him to me," Honey said. "McQueeny couldn't find Lake Michigan."

Honey drew his wife close.

"Jan's the only woman who could handle me," Honey said. "With all my transfers."

Jan smirked.

"Hell, I'm just like them Comanche squaws back in Texas," Jan said. "And J. Edgar Hoover, why, he the big chief. He says 'Move!' And we move. One dreary desert Resident Agency town after another. H.T. gone for weeks at a time. Po-lice gypsies, that's what it feels to this fat ole mama."

"Why does he call you 'Ranger Captain'?" Lee asked.

"'cause he always does," Jan said. "Come on, Lee, we gotta fatten you up."

Lee met the kids, Drew, ten, Daisy, seven and Bill, four.

They raced Santa Anna to the dinner table, grabbing at each other.

They sat down to a dinner stretched for Lee. Meatloaf, fresh corn, hush puppies and cold potato salad showed the tight Depression budget. Eskimo pies and coffee made the dessert. Lee wolfed it all down. Jan's home cooking beat anything that he had tasted in weeks.

CHAPTER 9: Winter 1932 – Spring 1933

BUREAU OF INVESTIGATION, MIDWEST REGION

Through that winter of 1932 and into the next spring, Lee would remember the driving.

A few words from the agent in charge, a pull of harsh coffee and the agents would go out, roaring along dirt roads on black nights with wet snow coming down on them.

The agents all used their own cars for Bureau business and they got used to the long drives.

There were only 260 Special Agents for the whole country. Some field offices stretched hundreds of miles apart.

Wherever the agents went, they drove through the heartbreak and misery of the Depression.

They penetrated factory towns where half the locals were unemployed and the other half worked at jobs for ten cents an hour. Families lived in packing crates, and thousands of lonely men roamed aimlessly, not having any job or family anymore.

When anyone stole a pound of Government scrap metal, the Bureau would slog through an investigation. When an ex-soldier who claimed to be disabled was faking his injuries, someone would squeal on him to the Bureau. Any bank teller who suspected her boss of embezzling funds could pick up the telephone and whisper to the agent on the complaint desk.

"You look too young, be a Government man," a gas pump jockey said to Lee. "Got anything to show me?"

Lee showed his credentials. The paragraph read 'Department of Justice, Bureau of Investigation.' Lee's photograph and signature lay alongside the words "This is to certify that on this date the bearer, whose photograph and signature appears heron, was regularly appointed as a Special Agent of the Department and as such is charged with the duty of investigating violations of the laws of the United States and collecting evidence in cases in which the United States is or may be a party in interest."

"Lot of five-dollar words," the gas pump jockey said. His round stubbled face squinted at the credentials again. "Do this little plastic card mean you're someone important?"

The agents interviewed judges, newspaper editors, civic-minded widows, sharecroppers and derelicts. They met every kind of lawman, Prohibition agents, county sheriffs, town marshals, Tribal Indian police and village constables. They would scribble notes, advise action and common law remedies, do title searches on pieces of property, serve subpoenas, survey boundary lines, and check automobile registrations. Nobody knew where all these facts were needed. But they funneled them to Washington.

The agents kept risking their lives on neglected roads in overworked cars, gambling on wheels that shot them into the night.

This is daffy, Lee thought. Some night they were going to hit a watermelon truck traveling without lights and get killed. They had no business racing around in the middle of the night, waiting for something to happen.

CHAPTER 10: Friday, June 16, 1933

HOT SPRINGS, ARKANSAS

It was a sweltering day in Hot Springs, Arkansas. Dogs lay belly up, tongues hanging out from the heat.

A fan working inside the White Front Cigar Store moved the hot air around as the barkeep opened up for the day. He folded back the big double doors and swept up.

Joe Lackey's breath chopped up from nerves, as he and his pals, F.S. "Frank" Smith and Otto Reed, entered. All wore summer suits and fanned themselves with their Panama hats. Joe was the youngest, a college type, with hawklike looks and wingy ears, while Frank was the oldest, with a round face sagging into his collar. Otto was the biggest, of the trio, with a mean hillbilly face and slicked-back thinning hair.

"Help you, gents?" the barkeep asked from behind the bar.

"Not just yet," Joe said.

Frank moved his own belly, scanned the cigar counter and whistled softly.

"Yeah," Frank said. "I'll have that package of Belvederes."

With a penknife, the barkeep cut the cord banding the cigars and exchanged them for a bill from Frank. He was fishing out change from the till when the back room door opened.

A runty guy, dressed in expensive golf clothes and wearing gold glasses, his dark hair combed into a pompadour, came out of the back room, sucking on a bottle of 3.2 beer.

"Morning, Mr. Moore," the barkeep said.

Before the man even had chance to respond, Joe grabbed the man by an arm. Frank dropped the bundle and cigars rolled across the floor. He gripped the man's other arm.

The barkeep reared back. His hands reached for a sawed-off shotgun under the counter.

Otto snaked a Colt horse pistol from under his suit jacket.

"Don't try for it, 'bo," Otto said.

The barkeep froze.

"Mr. Moore, I ain't got nothing to do with this," the barkeep said.

"Yeah, right," the man said. He looked mad. "Lemme remember your face."

Joe and Otto dragged the runty guy out of the store and onto Central Avenue.

A big black Buick was parked at the curb. Frank slid into the driver's seat. Joe and Otto, still holding the horse pistol, wrestled the man into the back seat.

The car screeched off down Central as the barkeep ran into the street with his sawed-off shotgun. He triggered a blast that woke up the quiet street but missed the Buick by inches.

The man breathed heavily, looking from side at his captors.

"C'mon, you guys," he pleaded. "I'm Charles Moore, a respectable citizen. You're messing with the wrong fella. Let me out, and we'll forget about it."

"Bureau of Investigation, Department of Justice," Joe said.

He fumbled handcuffs out of his suit jacket pocket.

When the man tried to yank back his hands, Joe took his right arm and handcuffed both the gangster's wrists.

"Frank Nash," Joe continued. "You're under arrest for knowingly escaping custody from United States Prison, Leavenworth. I'm Special Agent Lackey, and Special Agent Smith is wheeling us."

Otto held the horse pistol against the man's back. With his free hand he lifted the pompadour. It came off in his hand.

"Easy with that toupee," Nash said. "I paid three C-notes for that in Chi,"

"We know all about you, Nash," Joe said.

He looked between Joe and Otto and sighed.

"Okay, I'm Nash. I guess you boys got me good."

"Then you won't mind if we call you 'Jelly', do you?" Joe asked.

"All my friends do."

"For 'Jellybean'?"

Nash grinned at the suggestion.

"For my professional associations," Nash said.

"Jelly" was slang for the blasting gelatin robbers used to blow open safes.

"Who are you boys again? " Nash asked.

Joe laughed. His big ears waggled.

"Us?" he asked. "Why, we're the poor, miserable, unknown agents of the Bureau of Investigation and just closed out our investigation by arresting you."

"'Bureau of Investigation'? G-men?! You boys can't arrest me. It ain't legal at all."

"Don't worry, 'bo." Otto holstered his horse pistol. "I'm Chief Reed, McAlester, Oklahoma po-lice, and I say it's legal."

"You've changed your looks considerably, Jelly," Joe observed.

"Wouldn't you?"

"Glasses. Moustache. Toupee to cover the old chrome dome. Not even your mother would recognize you."

"Your college boy buddy didn't. The fish wrappers said Ray Caffrey from your outfit spotted me but didn't snap in time. Too bad, he came up empty-handed."

"You'll see Ray again, Jelly. He's meeting us at the station and you can reminisce about old times on your way back to Leavenworth."

The car was passing out of Hot Springs.

"We'll see, gentlemen. Time will tell," Nash said, "It's a long way to Leavenworth, boys. And there's lots of bad law in this state."

"I'll take the wheel now," Joe said.

"This Grandpop ain't tuckered out yet," Frank said.

"Hell, us country Texas boys can keep the car flying along the dirt," Joe said. "All the way to Little Rock."

As they came around a curve outside of Benton, Arkansas, Joe hit the brakes. A roadster marked "Sheriff's Department" blocked the road. Winchesters pointed over the roadster's hood.

A pot-bellied granddad with a sheriff's star stood in front, holding a scattergun on the Buick. Joe smelled his own sweat.

"Here's some of that bad law," Frank muttered. He jounced Nash to the floorboards and held a hand on him.

Otto stepped out of the rear door, keeping his hands high and visible. "Police officer!" he bellowed. "I'm Chief Reed of McAlester bringing in a fugitive!"

The granddad with the star came up crabwise, the scattergun held tight against his hip.

"Show me."

Otto opened his wallet with the heavy gold chief's badge pinned to the leather.

"Just made the arrest this morning. Didn't have time to notify the police in Hot Springs."

"You bagged someone in Hot Springs? "the sheriff asked. "Shoot. Nobody gets arrested in Hot Springs. Crooks own that town and every copper in it."

"That's why I didn't wait around," Otto said. Joe heard him slur his country accent thicker, trying to seem harmless to win them over.

"Hot Springs is a hideout town," one of the deputies said. "Maybe you didn't know it, being a dumb Okie."

"Says which?" Otto asked.

"Who else is in that machine with you? "

"Department of Justice men. They got the paper on our bird."

"Sheriff, the federals can't do that here," the deputy said. "Never could. We got to hold them for Hot Springs. They squawked this as a kidnap."

The sheriff scanned Otto with rheumy blue eyes set in his loser's face. The deputies waited.

Otto returned the stare with an angry face.

"The hell with Hot Springs," the sheriff finally said. "I live on my pay. So long, chief. Godspeed."

Joe gunned the Buick out.

●

"I want to get out of this state alive," Nash said.

"You and me both," Frank answered.

"It'll be like that all along the way," the prisoner continued, "locals trying to spring me. You know all these places are bought and paid for. Nobody big gets arrested and brought out of Hot Springs. They can pick you off at the next roadblock or one by one on the cat roads. Law posses vanish in the Ozarks all the time. Never seen again."

"Sounds pretty risky," said Joe. "Maybe we should get the hell out of here."

"Drop me off by the side of the road," said Nash. "I'll guarantee safety for all of us."

"He's right about this area being bought and sold," Otto said. "You boys be glad you got a local with you."

"You federals got no cannons," Nash shook his bald head. "You're gonna need them."

"Write your congressman," Joe told him.

Everyone's face tensed up.

"I'm loaning them my guns," Otto said. "And whatever they might pick up lying around. I dang sure don't wanna know."

"So what you suggest?" Frank asked.

"Take State Road 6 through the Ouachita. Oldest National Forest in the South. Not a whole lot living there other than coons and bears. Then we pick up Highway 71 straight into Fort Smith."

"If they don't exterminate us," Nash observed.

Nash was someone rare in the Depression, a college-educated gangster.

"Say, Jelly, did you really pull that train robbery with the Spencer gang?"

"Always wanted to rob a train. It was a challenge. Just like you always wanted to grab a big name fugitive." Nash said.

He rested his bald head on the back of the seat.

"In my business, you gotta have brains 'cause you never know what the next challenge is gonna come from. Like my 25-year bit at Leavenworth. The deputy warden liked me and made me his house chef. I checked out a three-volume set of Shakespeare plays from the prison library and told the librarian I was gonna to see those plays in a real theater.

"He said that would never happen. The next day, I told the deputy warden that the kitchen needed more cinnamon. He told me walk into town to get it. Took the Shakespeare with me, too. I never went back."

Frank shook his graying head.

"No wonder you can con everyone," Frank said. "You're a card. Why were you in Leavenworth?"

"Oh, a killing." Nash paused and thought hard. "Can't remember which one. But I didn't do it."

The summer daylight was fading into dusk as they approached Fort Smith, Arkansas. It was still more than 300 long miles through the Ozarks to Leavenworth, Kansas, and the trio agreed that it would be far more dangerous on the roads when night fell.

●

They scored a quick meal of black coffee and hush puppies from a roadside stand in Fort Smith. Frank hunkered on the running board, eating as he looked out at the Ozarks.

Guarded by Otto, Nash ate in the back seat.

Joe set his plate of hush puppies on the plate.

"I can't eat," Joe said. "It's bad when us government men got to hide from other coppers. The crooks are running the countryside and nobody cares. The newspapers and the taxpayers tolerate them.

"I know that everyone wants to forget the Depression. The only people these days who've got cash are bankers and bandits. The bad guys are the only ones giving it away to the folks who got none."

Joe strolled over to a country store and asked a clerk, her face lined from too much time in the Arkansas sun, if he could make a collect call.

She eyed him as Joe dialed the operator.

He gave her number, and waited until she made sure that someone else would pay for it.

Eye on the woman, he tried sounding cheery. The Kansas City Special Agent in Charge, the SAC, a fast talker named Reed Vetterli, answered on the night-time phone line.

"Howdy, boss. Caught that big fish I've been trying to hook for years. But I'm afraid it might get a little stale by the time I get it to the icebox. Got any ideas?"

They knew that somebody could be listening in, on a country phone line.

"You don't know how lucky you were to get him out of Hot Springs," Vetterli said. "It's safer to put the fish on a train. The Missouri Pacific will bring you into Union Station here at 7:15 in the morning. We'll have you covered, and we'll drive the fish out to Leavenworth in time for lunch."

"You'll meet us?" Joe asked.

"Sure. Rules say that we have to notify the local fishermen. But we can't trust them. Too many thumbs on the scale. So I'll be there with Ray Caffrey."

"Got it."

He hung up. The clerk still stared.

He bought a sack full of Eskimo Pies and walked outside.

•

Joe nodded to Frank, and got behind the wheel. Otto eased his bulk, holding his horse pistol into the back seat beside Nash. Frank slid in from the other side.

"What's Kansas City like?" Joe asked.

"Last big town you pass through before going west. It's a cow town," said Nash. "Businessmen wear boots and cowboy hats. Biggest industry is meat packing from the slaughterhouses."

"I hope they don't pack us," Otto said.

The car fell quiet, the loudest sound the whooshing of the tires. Everyone looked at everyone else.

They had reached the outskirts of Fort Smith. The street-lights began.

•

In the Kansas City Field Office hallway, Vetterli stopped a young agent with a round Irish choirboy's face and glossy black hair.

"Say, Caffrey," he asked. "We're all working late tonight. How long did you trail Jelly Nash last year?"

"About two months, boss." Caffrey said. "Old Jelly is slippery. Popping up all over the state, and I kept hitting the towns a day or so after he left. I lived in the Chevy and didn't see Regina or my son, Jimmie, for weeks. Then, we got three of his cronies in the golf course arrests, but Nash slid out of sight."

"The Bureau's got Nash now," Vetterli said, slapping Caffrey's shoulder. "Arrested by our fellers and taken out of Hot Springs.

He's being brought into Union Station tomorrow morning. You've been cooped up in the office all week, Ray, so this'll be a nice change for you. What do you say we both go out down to the station together and pick up Nash? "

CHAPTER 11: Saturday, June 17, 1933

KANSAS CITY, MISSOURI

In the morning, the group holding Nash rode into Kansas City's Union Station on the Missouri Pacific train. Sunlight buttered their stateroom. Joe and Frank stretched and yawned while Pullman porters chatted with family groups in the corridor.

All night long, a song from years ago had been playing inside Joe's head.

> "O! The refrigerator will never replace the ice-man.
> Two tongs and a hammer will do the best that we can!"

He hummed what he could remember as he checked Nash's handcuffed hands and put Nash's toupee back on over his bald head.

"That rug is worth every penny you paid for it, Jelly." Frank said. "Makes you look like a man of distinction."

"Now, boys," Nash grinned. "Quit your joshing, fellas, you're still young. You got your hair."

Otto broke out a sawed-off pump shotgun from under his car coat and held it down by his thigh. He pushed open the door to the corridor and peeked out.

"You can get yourself some tonic mailed into Leavenworth," Otto said. "Some cure-all to put the follicles back in."

Frank and Joe brought Nash out into the corridor as the train was slowing down. Otto walked behind, shotgun on his shoulder as though he were hunting. Nash was trying to cover the cuffs with his handkerchief.

"Frank, take my six-inch and hold it down by your leg," Otto said. "Something don't feel right here."

"'O! The refrigerator'," Joe thought.

Caffrey already had his Chevy at the station entrance, with the engine running. Vetterli stood in the station parking lot, watching.

Union Station was crowded with groups of farmers in overalls, tourists in Panama hats and Catholic nuns in their black and white habits.

A marked police car pulled up while the agents brought Nash off the train and onto the platform. The gilt six-point star stood out against the cream-colored door. A red spotlight nested over the driver's door. Two men in wrinkled dusty suits got out.

"Grooms and Hermanson, Burglary Detail," the younger cop said. "You called for a prisoner escort?"

"Had to," Vetterli muttered. "Regulations."

Joe saw Caffrey's mouth turn down as he scanned the burglary cops.

"Morning, Jelly," Caffrey patted Nash on the arm. "Good to see you. It's been a while."

The group moved over to the Chevy in the parking lot.

"Get in the front seat, Jelly," Caffrey said.

Joe got in the back.

"Up! Up! Get 'em up!"

A Tommy gun ripped. Someone big came from behind a parked car, flames spurting out. Another gunner opened up. Noise hammered Joe's ears.

"Refrigerator!" Joe thought.

Otto's shotgun boomed. Joe felt slugs rip into him. He smelled rubber upholstery and blood. Noise blotted out everything.

Caffrey went down, his face blasted open. The station roared with gunfire. The KC coppers fell, hats blown back by the gunfire. Nash's head whipped back, and the bloody toupee fell off. Men screamed over the Tommy noise.

Frank lay flat inside the car, untouched. The nuns ran shrieking through the lot. Vetterli spun to the hot pavement, feeling his palms smack. A car swung in front of the Chevy, and the big Tommygunner jumped in. A cop in blue came racing through the station doors and fumbled out his service gun in a clumsy draw.

"Shoot the fat man!" a woman screeched.

The cop in blue triggered a long, desperate shot at the big gunner.

The other Tommy opened up and the cop ducked. Vetterli saw the big gunner, big as Babe Ruth with the same round face, as the car tore away.

Joe lay moaning in the car. Vetterli got to his feet, stumbling against one of the dead cops. Blood ran like a syrup around the car. Frank arose from the floor. Joe touched Frank's arm. Joe's fingertips felt nothing. Joe felt numb everywhere. Blood ran down his back.

The cop in blue ran up, smoky gun still in his hand.

"Who are you people?" he gasped.

●

At the Chicago office, a dozen agents grouped in the bullpen interviewing citizens and answering phones. Lee was handwriting a Federal Document 302 report when Honey entered the bullpen.

"Get ready to work, kid. The boss is coming in."

Melvin Purvis, the Chicago Special Agent in Charge, swept inside. The SAC was small, barely five-foot four and delicately built. He looked like a country boy with a bony, hungry face. He rapped a table ashtray. The agents stopped talking, and the sitting ones stood.

"Gentlemen," he said, "we've got a big shooting in Kansas City. At least one Bureau agent is dead on the scene. I want the following men in my office in five minutes, ready to leave for Kansas City. Suran, Hollis, Bisbee, Ross, McQueeny, Winstead and Laughlin. And one more. Let me see."

Lee felt scared. He wanted to stay here.

Roy Suran hulked over Purvis, a husky kid with pearly teeth that seemed too big for his mouth, a football fullback and honor student from George Washington University Law School. That had been Director Hoover's school. Dozens of their best grads applied for the Bureau.

Herman Hollis showed a slim, scholarly face like a scientist always hunting more facts. His dark eyes always seemed to look through you. But Hollis was a lawyer who could shoot. His sharpshooting amazed his hunting buddies. Whenever Purvis authorized an agent to be armed, he looked to Hollis first.

Charlie Winstead combed silver-gray hair with his fingers and wore cowboy boots that marked him as a Texan. He and Honey had rangered in the same company, swapping lies about their scars.

"And Childress," Purvis finished.

The news startled Lee. Lee glanced at Honey. Honey nodded. His face showed nothing.

"The rest of you hit the bricks right now. Get out and talk to your informants. In my absence, ASAC Pedersen will be in charge."

•

The selected agents rummaged through the desk drawers and threw handcuffs, extra razors, and nickel notebooks into their bulging briefcases.

"Purvis is goofy," Homer Bisbee said in his dull monotone. Bristly hair stuck up from his pale face. He rocked his soft body in the chair and bumped his knee on the desk. "Purvis said to talk to your informants'? I don't have any informants. What makes him think we do police work here?"

"I can't imagine," Cecil Laughlin said. Cecil was dapper in a white linen suit. His pink shirt gleamed in the sunlight. He wore his fair hair parted in the middle, plastered down. "He couldn't get that impression looking at you, Homer Bisbee. Or watching you avoid work."

Homer Bisbee scratched himself.

"Let me make it easy for you to understand, Homer Bisbee," Cecil Laughlin said. "There's an agent dead. He could have been you. Or any one of us."

"Not me, Cecil. I don't get paid enough."

Honey came over while Homer Bisbee was bent over to get his briefcase.

"Hey, Cecil?" Honey pointed at Homer Bisbee's bottom. "Would you?"

Cecil Laughlin looked at Homer Bisbee's gray flannel bottom.

"No, I would not," he answered.

"Would you what?" Homer Bisbee asked.

"Nothing, Homer," Honey said. "Just a little joke I picked up while guarding prisoners down in Texas."

"Prison love," Cecil hissed. "With a handful of grease. Strong men, Homer Bisbee, they fight over a junior like you."

"Sometimes I can't even understand your words," Homer Bisbee said.

"From way up the mountain in Vermont. You think my accent is thick? You should try understanding my farmer uncle, who talks like he has marbles in his mouth."

"Let Kansas City Field Office handle this," McQueeny said. "I got too much work already."

"Yeah," Cecil said. "That's why you take two-hour lunches."

Lee stood with his briefcase, feeling left out.

"Hey, Honey, am I going with you two on the flight?" Lee asked.

"Damn straight." Honey snapped his carpet bag shut.

"Why?" Lee asked, still uncertain.

"Cecil and I are going because we used to be partners. We requested you in case anything big broke. Cecil wanted to be a doctor, but he flunked the handwriting course. We need someone to write up reports legibly enough for Purvis to read."

"At least I know how to read and write," Cecil said.

"So you DID learn something at Yale. Bow-wow! Bow-wow!" Honey roared out the old football cheer. "Bulldog Yale!"

•

Purvis paused on the garage stairs, his fedora slanted, his elegant collar loose. He twirled the stub of a French cigarette between his fingers as he watched the agents pile into their cars.

"Are we bringing McQueeny?" Lee asked.

"What for?" Cecil said. "Ballast?"

"You're a Yale grad?" Lee asked Cecil.

"Law graduate," Cecil said. "Worked as a New Haven Deputy Taxi Constable to make tuition payments. It was just supposed to be a lark for my final year."

"It still is, to you," Honey said. "My little Yalie."

"Sure, it is," Cecil said. "I only turned G-man to meet women."

"Who calls us 'G-men?'" Lee asked.

"Machine Gun Kelly calls us that when he's raising hell in Tulsa," Cecil said. "It stands for 'Government men.'"

"Keep it in your pants, Cecil," Honey said. "Today, we work, for real in the field. For a change. Like we should have been doing all along."

•

Lee and Honey rode in Cecil's family car along Michigan Avenue. Cecil drove like a maniac, snarling at the traffic from behind the wheel.

"That damn ribbon clerk Purvis doesn't know cops. Neither does our Director, old J. Edgar Hoover. They got no right to send us to Godforsaken places to make arrests with borrowed guns. And no bosses with guts."

"Jesus, Cecil," Honey murmured. "Tell it to the Marines."

Cecil pointed at Lee.

"Is this kid regular, Honey? Can I talk in front of him?"

"If you can't, it's too late now."

"Say, Childress, are you real? Are you for real?"

Cecil's lip curled and his green eyes flashed.

Lee did not know what to say.

"Real. A real cop," Cecil said. He hit the horn. "What did you do before?"

"Law school."

"Ain't real. Not real. No real cops here," Cecil said to himself. "Just me and Honey. The only ones."

Cecil looked over at the chunky redhead and a smile played around his mouth.

"Honey," he said. "Ho-ney."

Cecil slammed to a stop in front of a hash house on Clark Street. The trio got out and stepped into the alley. Lee felt his breath quicken. His belly bucked like he might throw up.

"No talking now," Honey said. "But I'll show you how to arm yourselves without an act of Congress. Cheaply, on our pay."

Cecil kicked in a wooden door and they slammed into the hash house kitchen.

"Federal officers!" Honey bellowed. "Don't move! This is a raid!"

Four men were playing poker hands at the kitchen table. They looked like Italians to Lee, dark, with moustaches.

One tried to get past Cecil. Honey grabbed his hair and slammed his head into the greasy kitchen wall. Lee, giggling from nerves, took a long step and booted the table.

The men went down, tangled in their chairs. Cecil leaned over, grabbed one skinny bald man by the throat, and jerked a gun from the man's hip pocket.

Lee copied him. He palmed a heavy revolver from the man's wide stevedore's belt.

Honey got a third gun from the kitchen stove. He covered the kitchen while his partners went back through the alley.

"Nobody get cute!" Honey roared. "You egg-sucking dogs are all under arrest! There's a car outside the door. Get inside it and we're going downtown!"

Honey jumped back into the car's front seat next to Lee and Cecil. Without waiting, Cecil floored the car and drove them back down Clark Street. Lee's fingertips left sweat marks on the taped gun butt.

Cecil stopped in an alley.

"Let's divvy up, see what we got," Cecil panted. He held up a stubby automatic pistol. "Mauser pocket model. Bullet's too light. All you do with that is make someone mad. The other's some Dago pea shooter I can't even pronounce."

He pointed to Lee's gun.

"That's a sweet one, kid," Honey said. "Colt New Service .45 caliber. That bad rascal sawed down the barrel for an easy carry. Packs a hell of a punch. Any shooting, drop it and say it belonged to the other guy. Do the job right, and he won't be in a position to argue. Nobody will care, except maybe Purvis."

"Nervous Purvis, we call him," Cecil said.

"Okay, team," Honey said. "Let's fly to Kansas City and show the Director what we can do."

That night, Purvis and the agents flew a bumpy rough flight to Kansas City. Nobody talked much. They smoked and read case files.

Lee felt sick to his stomach. He had never flown in a plane before.

CHAPTER 12: Saturday June 17, 1933

KANSAS CITY, MISSOURI

Purvis led the agents to the train station from the airfield. Nobody was sleeping tonight,

Even at night, Union Station held the circus crowds that followed violent death in the Depression.

Lee saw hundreds of gawkers, wearing straw hats and fanning themselves against the night's heat, crowded through the parking lot.

Caffrey's Chevrolet was a wreck. Blood was splattered everywhere. Frank Nash's brains dripped from the dashboard.

The window glass crunched underfoot. A white sailor hat lay on the back seat, with the name "Jimmie Caffrey" inked inside the brim. KC cops in heavy blue serge uniforms pushed and bullied the crowd back from the car. They talked rough. They had lost two of their own.

Lee showed his credentials and ducked under the police rope. Vetterli was licking his fingers covered with a gooey Eskimo pie and balancing a steaming cup of coffee in his free hand.

"Melvin," Vetterli said. "I'm still shaking. Threw up already. Them coppers. Ray dead. Thought I was a goner."

"Thank God, Reed. Try telling me what you remember."

"I don't figure they planned on hitting Nash," Vetterli said. "I was standing at the rear and west side of Caffrey's car. The first gunner, the big guy, seemed to be standing on the running board of a car. The getaway car took off westward out of the station parking lot."

"How many shooters, Reed?"

"Two different Tommy guns. That I saw. And a third man was hunched over the seats as they left."

"Who's dead here?" Honey broke in. "Give me some names."

"Our man, Ray Caffrey, twenty-eight years old."

"You knew him?"

"The Bureau's small. I knew him."

Honey bit his lip and spat on the ground. His jaws worked.

"Also dead are two Kansas City dicks," Vetterli continued. "Ted Grooms and Frankie Hermanson. Reed, the police chief from somewhere in Oklahoma.

"Our agent, Joe Lackey, got hit bad. He's not dead yet but he's a helluva lot less alive than he ever was before. He lost consciousness in the ambulance going to Research Hospital. He'll be a cripple, if he lives. I got nicked in the arm and Smith, out of the Oklahoma City office, wasn't hit at all."

"That's a miracle," Purvis said. He scanned the car.

"The guy they were trying to free is dead, too. Convicted scum Frank Nash, who wasn't worth all this killing, anyway." Vetterli lowered his voice. "I've got Smith with a witness I want to keep away from the locals."

"The Director was very clear about that," Purvis said. "This is a Bureau investigation. He does not trust the Kansas City cops."

"No reason why he should," Vetterli said. "Grooms and Hermanson were burglary cops. They were given this assignment because they were the only squad car equipped with Tommy guns. But somebody took the Tommies out last night, while the car was in the police garage. Most KC cops can't put their shoes on in the dark."

"Okay, we're gonna go with Bureau practice and set up a Bureau Special command post." Purvis said. He spoke the word 'Bureau' lovingly, his South Carolina drawl thickening with emotion. "Have us check into the Weiss Hotel, across from the station plaza."

After they checked into the old-fashioned roomy hotel, painted in white and gold colors, they kept working.

The agents unpacked their briefcases. Purvis laid a police identification book on the dresser and set up a small blackboard in their suite.

"Why did they shoot?" Lee asked. "Does anybody know?"

"Some guys like to shoot and kill," Honey said.

"Let's see," Purvis stood like a lecturer in front of the agents and sketched the station scene with chalk. "The police chief had a shotgun, and it was fired. He may have shot Nash instead of letting him get sprung. Smith says he was a stubborn, honest, old-fashioned policeman –"

"Not like us," Honey said.

"– so maybe he decided they weren't going to get Nash. We have a lot of descriptions already. Dozens of witnesses. The station was packed. People say the killers looked like Machine Gun Kelly, Wilbur Underhill, Baby Face Nelson, Verne Miller or Harvey Bailey."

"Who are those fellas?" Lee asked.

"Those are criminals, mister lawyer," Honey said. "Bad jaspers. You're just a sprout so you don't know them yet. When you have more time on the job, you'll get to know them all."

"How would I know them? All I do is drive all night and file reports back at the office fiefdom."

"Up until today, that is," Honey said

"Listen up, gentlemen," Purvis said. "We have at least three shooters in this massacre. Two used Tommy guns with .45 caliber slugs. The third man used two different .45 revolvers. At the rate and the number of slugs the whole shooting took about forty seconds."

The door opened and Vetterli urged a middle-aged woman in. She wore a plain black dress that crisped in the heat and glasses dangling from a chain.

"Lottie West from Travellers Aid," said Vetterli, "She saw the big Tommy gunner hanging around the station before the shooting."

The woman tensed and Vetterli patted her arm.

"You've got nothing to fear. We'll protect you," he said.

Vetterli led Lottie to the dresser. She put on her glasses as he opened the police identification book. He flipped through photographs of scowling and scarred men. They were country gunmen. The photos mixed in with those of the dashing city mobsters. Profiles were on the left side, with a full face on the right.

Vetterli flipped over a picture of a mustached man wearing a battered fedora.

"Stop!" said Lottie.

She peered closer at and tapped a photograph in the middle of a row of similar ones. In the photo, a square-jawed big man wore a suit and patterned bowtie.

The agents paid close attention.

"That's him," she said. "That's the man who fired on the officers with a submachine gun."

Purvis approached the woman. "You're sure?"

"I have to remember people's faces, sonny. That's part of my job. This man was about thirty years old. He had a fat face, red complexion like he worked outdoors. Wore a dark blue suit with a white shirt and a turned-down Panama hat. He must have weighed at least 230 pounds."

Honey smiled at Purvis. He knew about witnesses from his years in the Bureau. This one would go right down the line and testify in court. She would put the man in the picture in the electric chair.

"We're not going to learn much about this killing for a while, boss," Honey said. "We've been pushed here and we're gonna have to push back hard. This case isn't getting closed out until every one of these killers is dead. And that may take months."

Purvis nodded. The hotel suite fell silent as he took the mug book from Lottie and slipped the photograph out of the sleeve. He held it up to show the agents.

"Pretty Boy Floyd," he said softly.

CHAPTER 13: Saturday, June 17, 1933
Later That Night

KANSAS CITY, MISSOURI

Lee was driving one rented car, Honey slouching in the passenger seat, checking a list of their stops. Cecil and Suran were teamed in another car. As Purvis drove his car, Bisbee fell asleep in the back seat.

Kansas City still crackled with the shock of the killings.

Newsboys hawked newspapers shouting, "Extra! Extra! Read all about the massacre at Union Station."

Suran had Cecil stop their car above the dark waters of the Missouri River. When Lee saw this in his rearview mirror, he too, pulled over and slowly backed up.

Suran stepped out of the car, bought a *Kansas City Star* and paced the sidewalk as he studied the article.

Honey also stepped out. A newsboy approached him.

"Paper, mister?" the newsboy asked. "

Honey nodded at Suran.

"I'll read his," Honey said.

"When I was a law-studying back at George Washington U.," Suran told Honey, "I was dating a peach of a girl, Caroline West.

Youngest of three beautiful sisters. Everyone in the Washington law world was sparking the West sisters. Corsages, yachts and picnics. Back then, Caroline was toiling as an ink-stained wretch, clerking in the Justice Department.

"She broke up with me to marry another young lawyer who joined the Bureau. That was Joe Lackey, from Cuero, Texas. Colonel Lackey's son. After training, I got Chicago Field Office under Purvis. Lackey and Caroline were sent to Oklahoma City."

"The papers say that Lackey had survived his operation," Suran said. "But he will live as a cripple. Two .45 slugs in his spine and a third one in his hip. I'm thinking about Caroline West. Sooner or later, Floyd is going to pay."

Honey returned to the front car with the newspaper. Suran slid in beside Cecil, and the pair of cars drove off into the sweltering night.

"I told my Ranger Captain," Honey said, "that I just flew out of town from Chicago. No need to mention Kansas City and worry her. By now, the whole country knows about Kansas City."

Lee let out the clutch and they rolled into the seedy riverfront alleys behind factories off West Third Street.

Honey pulled out a bottle of whiskey. He offered Lee a swig, and when Lee declined, took a deep gulp himself. He set the bottle in his lap and lit a wooden match with his thumbnail.

Police cars crisscrossed through the riverside streets. Some held uniformed men with pump guns on their laps.

Honey torched his cigar and sucked in a mouthful of smoke. He exhaled, took another swig of whiskey and pointed his elbow at a late-model car running without its headlights. The vehicle was packed with grim-faced men wearing fedoras. It nosed quietly down an alley.

Honey snorted. "Look at them po-lice suckers."

"Why suckers?"

"Even if they catch Floyd, the charges won't stick. Alibis will be bought, witnesses will leave town, someone else will confess and die in jail. This is Kansas City, kid. The fix is in. Purvis told me a joker named Tom Pendergast runs this town. His boy, Lazia, runs the Northside and the police captains just kind of curl up in Lazia's lap."

Headlights washed over Honey's red hair.

"Hot Springs, Kansas City and a dozen other cities got no law worth the name," Honey said.

"My Pop always said nobody respects police outfits," Lee said. "Even if they want to."

"Somehow Americans let their towns get like this. We got to fix it."

"You think the Bureau can?" Lee asked.

"Yup. Even with all our idiots buzzing around the office trying to tell us that water ain't wet. We are cleaner than any police outfit in the country. Some of us are seasoned types who just won't back down."

"You make us sound important. But sometimes I get the feeling that we're just doing what politicians tell us to do."

"It may look that way. But every cop has got to bend with the politicians to some degree. The Bureau. Texas Rangers. Even a one-man sheriff's office has got to be popular enough so people want it to continue working. You can't fight everyone. We've got to show all the good we can do."

"That's dangerous," Lee said.

"Damn right. We'll lose some men before people come around to our side. But this is our country, and I'm not giving it over to crooks just so I can live longer. Cecil and a few others feel like I do."

Honey's words made Lee's palms sweat, sitting in the dark car.

"Honey, I'm just sitting out this Depression," Lee said. "I didn't sign on for a war."

"Maybe you should slide out. Before things got too risky."

Lee's hands wetted and shook.

●

They made a few stops in speakeasies and poolhalls. Honey found the boss man in each place and pitched him a short speech about cooperation. Lee watched Honey and followed his lead.

The first speakeasy let them in and listened. They promised to call the Bureau if they heard anything.

Most places sneered at them.

One cornhusker squared off and put his hand on Honey. Honey grinned and tapped him with his folded *Kansas City Star.* The cornhusker dropped, whimpering.

Lee saw the metal pipe hidden inside Honey's newspaper.

Some bosses showed respect. Nobody wanted this kind of heat. But they had nothing to tell them.

•

Cecil and Suran kept wheeling through the stockyards. Their headlights picked out mangy dogs, filthy mutts chewing on bones.

"Puppies!" Cecil crooned. "Hi, nice puppy! Come here, boy."

One mutt growled. Suran tensed.

"Naw. Nice little puppy. I like dogs, Suran. If I could turn Purvis into a cocker spaniel, our relationship would probably improve."

Suran finger-tapped his own temple.

"Nice puppy, nice puppy." Cecil said. "Want to become a Melvin Purvis, nice puppy? Looks like this dog belonged to a girl I was dating in law school. I got to like the dog more than I liked her. When we broke up, I only missed the dog."

Then they took a break to park in an alley to smoke and slurp bad coffee.

Someone tapped on their window.

A husky young copper played a flashlight over the Buick interior. He was a big-boned, cowlicked country boy who looked out of place in his stiff serge uniform.

"You fellas have any business around here?"

"Yes, we do," Cecil said.

Cecil sounded like a gentleman telling the butler to run along.

"Department of Justice, officer." Suran flipped open his credentials case. "We're on assignment here."

"You might not want to be around here," he said. "It's pretty grim at night."

"We'll handle it okay," Cecil snapped. "Thanks for your worry and goodnight. Go tell your boss that we're down here investigating him."

"What're you shouting at me for?" the boy snapped back. "I got no boss. I don't have Tom Pendergast or Johnny Lazia telling me what to do, if that's what you mean. I got a mean sergeant who don't like me. I do my job and I do it clean.

"I'm not in with the ready-money boys. That's why I'm in an alley, working nights. You ever try it? You know what it's like when your feet hurt every day? And you can't sit down. You can't smoke. And nothing ever happens on your post. And even if it does, you can't do a thing about it."

The patrolman took off his hat and looked as if he might throw it away.

"G-men, I don't like what happened at the station today," he said. "We usually have three cars to escort a prisoner, not just one. And one car that mysteriously didn't have no Thompsons. It stinks. But I'm just one man.

"If the bosses will sacrifice two married detectives to keep doing business as usual, what'll they do to me? These crooks got the money and the juice.

"They got automatic guns, cars that'll sixty-five easy. We got roller skate clunkers that fall apart at forty. We buy our own equipment, get no training, no days off, .38s that are fifty years old. So I'm a jerk for trying to do my job. Let them have the goddamn town."

CHAPTER 14: Sunday, June 18, 1933

KANSAS CITY, MISSOURI

At three o'clock in the morning, Purvis got a telephone call in his hotel room. The caller said that one of the gunners was at 6612 Edgevale road in the Armour Hills district. Then he hung up the phone.

Purvis rousted everyone out of bed and told them to meet him near the house on Edgevale at a quarter to four in the morning.

The agents met and talked in whispers on the quiet, residential street.

"We look like college boys planning a panty raid on a girl's dorm," McQueeny said.

"Last year, some of us were," Lee answered.

As Special Agent in Charge, Purvis would lead the raid. Winstead and Honey were the most experienced ex-policemen in the group so they would enter the house first. Purvis doled out two handguns to them from a satchel.

"It's about time we got fully dressed," Honey said. "Mr. Purvis, you're arming us for real?"

"Mr. Purvis, these are just .25 caliber automatics," Hollis

said. "Popguns. Got no real punch. Is Washington trying to get us killed?"

"Those go back in the bag when we're done here," Purvis snapped. "Washington says that nobody knows if it's legal or not."

"That's Washington for you," Honey said.

"So use it only in defense of life." Purvis said. "Or both of us may wind up as federal prisoners ourselves."

"How can you live like that?" Lee muttered.

"What else can you do?" Honey asked. "If bosses had guts, they wouldn't be bosses."

"Say what, Special Agent Ross?" Purvis asked.

"Nothing, boss. Just schooling the youngster here."

"You others would keep watch from the street and alley-way," Purvis said. "I'll deal with you later, Ross."

The covering party stayed in front. The raiders moved through the back yard to the white frame suburban house.

It had a wooden rear door with glass window panes at the top. The agents waited and listened.

Lee's hands shook. He jammed them in his pockets.

Purvis kicked in the back door.

The wood splintered and the door went in. Honey entered while the glass was still falling.

Winstead followed, covering the room with a Colt Peacemaker, spur hammer back, gripped in both hands. It was his own hidden gun.

Lee came up the driveway to the back door, ready to drop and roll at the first shot.

The agents swept through the house and saw they had just missed someone.

Red beans and cabbage were still warm on the stove. There was a glass jar of moonshine and a shot glass still wet on the table.

Nobody had cleaned the dusty living room in years. A broken chair leaned against the wall. Heavy black curtains sagged.

•

"Our tipster said that Verne Miller rented this place," Purvis said. "Some of you may know him."

"Not much, boss," McQueeny said. "Tell us."

"Verne learned to use a machine gun with the AEF in the World War," Purvis said. "His war record cinched his election as Sheriff of Beadle County, South Dakota. He got elected sheriff and served for years. Then they checked the county funds. Some money had grown feet and beat it down the street. Auditors said Miller took it. Miller claimed it was a political frame-up."

●

Still leading, Purvis entered the bedroom.

Clips for a .45 were under the mussed double bed.

Winstead found three Hamm's beer bottles under the bed. He bundled them into a paper bag from his pocket. They might show some fingerprints.

Honey pointed to the leather golf bag in the corner.

"Looks more and more like Verne Miller lived here," he said. "That golf bag is old Verne's trademark."

"Come on, Ross," Purvis said. "A lot of people play golf."

"Remember the descriptions we got from that cop? And the bootblack at the station? They both say one of the killers was five-eight, 150, blond hair and dressed like a banker. That says Verne Miller to me."

Purvis nodded. "It could be. It's possible. But the Director says we have to listen to Vetterli on the subjects' descriptions. And our tipster could be wrong. So keep an open mind."

●

They went outside, still looking for clues.

"I wish I knew why they started shooting today," Purvis said. "Or who started shooting."

"We'll never know," Honey's face flushed. "Except that it was a police set-up. There's no reason for Ray and them boys to be lying dead right now. We don't share information with the cops on this one."

"We don't share on any of them," Lee spoke up. "Too many cops are controlled. I don't care what the Director wants us to think. We're running the investigation, not him. You all heard that woman identify Floyd. Floyd did the shooting here today. There's no reason why we should think differently."

Purvis and Honey stared at him, startled. Purvis twitched, his clear gray eyes troubled. He slanted his straw hat and shot his cuffs.

He pointed out houses where the agents should conduct interviews. The exhausted men walked down Edgevale Road, knocking on doors and whipping out their credentials.

Dogs began barking and windows scraped up in the sultry night.

•

Daybreak came at five, and Purvis called off the street canvass. "We'll all meet at noon in my room."

Heads bobbing from exhaustion, the agents drifted back to their parked cars.

•

In the gray daylight, Lee was driving Honey back to the hotel. "Turn left!" Honey said.

"This isn't the way to the hotel."

"Just do it," said Honey.

Lee did as instructed and soon found himself in the waterfront along the West Bottoms.

Honey retrieved his whiskey bottle from under the seat and drank to settle his nerves. His friend Ray had been chopped into dog meat by a gunman, leaving behind a wife and a six-year old son.

Honey directed Lee into an alley he remembered from other times in KC. Happier times. They locked their stolen guns and credentials inside the trunk.

Honey took Lee into a cat house where the bootleg whiskey and women were still working their nighttime magic in the morning. Lee was skittish about going inside a cat house for the first time.

"Honey, I can't drink," Lee said.

"You want to learn your job, you better start now," Honey said. "I'll teach you what you need to survive. But we gotta drink first."

Honey was starting to relax and enjoy himself as the whiskey curled and burred Lee's tongue.

Girls lounged along the bar. A redhead with creamy skin and a fine, long-legged body winked at Honey. Healthy blonde girls just off the farm, their country talk clashing with their black dresses and cigarette holders.

Honey and Lee dove into the whiskey and finished the job by belting down a few extra, to keep away the nightmares.

The redhead picked Lee as a challenge.

"Hi, cute little boy," she said. She curled onto his lap like a big cat. "My name's Boogie-Woogie."

Boogie-Woogie began working on Lee's body below the belt.

Lee pushed her off and stepped clear.

"Now, there's no need for that," he said.

"Speak for yourself," Honey giggled.

He clinked glasses with a blonde dancer with racoony dark eyes.

"You remind me of a gal in Lubbock," Honey said. "So pretty. Broke a chair over her man's head and took her parking in the backyard."

He and the blonde clicked glasses again.

The room began to swim in Lee's eyes. Wicked wall spins, like the rummies said.

Boogie-Woogie blew on Lee's ear, and whispered.

"I can make you forget all the gals you know," she said. "Got special tricks."

Lee downed another glass of hooch.

The noise of the cat house piano and other drinkers rose and fell around him.

Lee stepped near Honey. Boogie-Woogie trailed.

"We're lawyers and accountants," Honey said to the blonde. "The best minds in the world are shysters and bean-counters. Director says so. In KC for a convention. Can't have fun without professional types like us in your party."

"Pro-fessional," Lee stressed. "Bosses love that word."

●

When Lee woke up, he was in bed with Boogie-Woogie. He shivered. His bones clacked as he swung his feet onto the floor. Last night's clothes lay wrestled there.

"You were bad-dreaming?" she asked.

"Back in Nebraska with the family," he whispered. "Now I don't want to leave the dream. Or the bed with you in it."

"What are you talking?"

"Face all that mess as a fake. Honey is cuckoo. I'll resign by telegram from this bed."

Boogie-Woogie grumbled and slipped back to sleep.

Lee simpered and dropped his head back on the pillow. Sleep came back over him and his dream about Nebraska returned. He could hear his mother calling to him.

CHAPTER 15: Monday, June 19, 1933

MEXICO CITY, MEXICO

It was just before full daybreak when Generalissimo Guillermo, Commandant of Police for Mexico City, reviewed his men. He was dressed in his finest dark green uniform, with a black mourning band sewn over his gold breast badge. His black boots shone as he snapped out a long salute.

The buttery soft bugle call of *El Deguello* poured over the crisp air. The music mourned the cutting of throats and innocent lives lost. Mexican buglers had played it at the Alamo battle.

Five thousand of his policemen came to attention, returning his salute and holding it. A few were *Maki* Indians, unable to read or write, with high cheekbones and big heads. Some looked like pudgy bankers' sons, their soft lives ruined by the Depression. They all knew that a group of Yanqui policemen had been massacred in Kansas City the day before. Guillermo knew he would be criticized by his politicians and civilians for honoring the dead police of another country.

This assembly would seem pointless to a civilian. But a cop would understand. The police had no family except for each other. When one of them died, all the others felt it.

The policemen stood for one minute in silent tribute to their fallen comrades. *El Deguello* spun out the tune.

CHAPTER 16: Monday, June 19, 1933
That Afternoon

KANSAS CITY, MISSOURI

That afternoon, after the noon meeting, Purvis brought the agents to Joe Lackey's room in St. Joseph Hospital. Lackey lay safe there. Vetterli said that Tom Pendergast controlled all the other hospitals for White folks. The Indians, Mexicans and Blacks had their own hospital.

All the agents except Homer Bisbee grouped around Joe Lackey, lying in his hospital bed.

Homer Bisbee settled his squishy body into the only chair. He burped.

"Excuse me," he muttered.

Joe Lackey, the reedy agent, the cowboy turned lawyer turned invalid, looked about nineteen. His dark hair was wet with sweat, and his face was unshaven. Every breath he took looked painful. Bandages crossed his whole upper body. Bottled fluids snaked into him.

"Joe, they got the slug out of your hip," Vetterli said. "They're saying that if you keep going fine like this, you'll dance the Charleston out of here. Your average fella would be graveyard dead by now."

"Like I told you, boss," Joe whispered. "Us Texans is tough. Right, Honey?"

"Too tough to die," Honey said.

"We boys are going to find the morphodites that did this," Vetterli said, "and put them down."

"No politics now?" Joe whispered. "Hey, Honey. I wish. But we ain't real cops."

"Just watch us," Honey said.

Lee stepped closer to the bed.

Purvis shook his head and thumbed him back.

"Let them talk, Mr. Childress," Purvis said. "The rest of us will hold our mud."

"Old Verne Miller was one of those bastards, Joe," Vetterli said. Never the same after he lost his sheriff's badge."

"And his marbles, too," Honey said. "He loves to drink that rye whiskey. He can put away two quarts a day. Maybe that's why he started shooting. We've got him identified already, by witnesses. We got him good enough for trial right now."

"Joe, a letter came in the mail for you this morning," Vetterli said. He took out a long government envelope.

"I want to read it here. So these guys know what it means, what you and Ray and the others have done."

The letter was dated June 18, 1933.

> John Edgar Hoover
> Director
> U.S. Bureau of Investigation
> Department of Justice
> Washington, D.C.

Mr. F.J. Lackey,
c/o Special Agent in Charge
United States Bureau of Investigation
905 Federal Reserve Bank Building
Kansas City, Missouri.

Dear Mr. Lackey:

The last few days have, indeed, been a nightmare to us all and I have been hoping and praying that your condition would not prove as serious as was first believed.

Today, when I received word from the Kansas City office of the very satisfactory progress you have made toward a recovery, it was, indeed, a most consoling message, and relieved me considerably from the worry which I had over your condition

I want to take this occasion to express to you, not only as Director of this Bureau but also as a close personal friend, my privilege and pleasure in being able to claim an acquaintanceship and friendship with one who has carved for himself a niche in the Hall of Courage which all of us may well be proud of and which may serve as our ideal.

It, of course, did not take the tragic events of last Saturday morning to inform me as to the sterling, courageous character which you possess, but the events of that morning have served to emblazon not only in the eyes of all your associates and friends, but in the eyes of the entire nation, the type of courage typical of a Special Agent of the United States Bureau of Investigation, and of this, I know, you are justly proud.

I thank God that we lost but one man in this battle, and that in a short time you will be back with us again carrying on as I know you will even more vigorously than ever in the interest of law enforcement.

It is needless for me to say to you that no time, money or labor will be spared toward bringing about the apprehension of the individuals responsible for the cowardly and despicable act of last Saturday morning. They must be exterminated and must be exterminated by us, and to this we are dedicating ourselves.

Let me urge that you by no means be concerned about your condition, for all of the care and attention will be given you, and all we are looking forward to is your early return and complete recovery. If there is any service I can be to you, either personally or officially, do not hesitate to command me.

With expressions of my best regards, I am,
Sincerely yours,
J. Edgar Hoover

The hospital room hushed.

"If the Director wants to be of service," Joe whispered, "he should gun us up, proper, with Tommy guns and pump shotguns. I'm finished, Mr. Vetterli. I know I'm never going to walk again. And other agents will get crippled, so long as we try to push our way into police work."

"Some of the people want these towns cleaned up, Joe."

"'The people'? Hell, they don't even know who we are."

•

That afternoon, the squad fretted in Honey's hotel room, Their feet tapped the carpet, ready to hit the bricks,

"So far, we ain't got enough to arrest nobody," Cecil said.

Purvis was in his own room, on a phone call to J. Edgar Hoover.

Around 5:30, Purvis entered without knocking, catching Bisbee asleep again.

Purvis pretended not to notice Bisbee.

"He don't wanna know," McQueeny muttered.

"All right, gentlemen," Purvis said. "Ross and Laughlin, I'm assigning you to go into Oklahoma to track down Pretty Boy Floyd. The rest of us will remain here in Kansas City till we locate Verne Miller."

"The fingerprints on the Edgevale beer bottles belong to a hoodlum named Adam Richetti. We can assume he is the third shooter in the Massacre."

"Boss, Cecil and I need another agent," Honey said. "A relief man for driving and stakeouts. We need a scribbler for the reports, too. Me and the English language, we old sparring partners, with nobody winning. Washington can't read Texas."

"We need our experienced agents, Ross."

"Then give us a green one. Give us Childress."

"They grow no greener," Bisbee said.

Lee colored and glared at Bisbee.

"His reports read okay," Honey said. "They make sense, even to me. And the reports on this one are going straight to the Director."

"I'll check," Purvis said.

McQueeny came over next to Lee, dropping into one of the suite's armchairs.

"The boss should not send you out on this case," McQueeny said. He spoke low so nobody else could hear. "It's a rigged game. Those Tommy guns that Grooms and Hermanson were supposed to have? They were taken out of their car, the so-called 'hot-shot' car, and stashed at Johnny Lazia's North Side Club. So a word to the wise, young Childress –"

"Maybe later," Lee said.

"Maybe now. There may not be another time."

Homer Bisbee dropped his credentials case on the floor.

"I learned how to survive sea changes in the body politic," McQueeny said. "There's a time to fight and a time to walk away. We are briefcase agents with no guns, real training, respect or authority. When it comes to police work, this Bureau better walk away. Or else we'll wind up like Lackey."

"I've decided you can have Childress," Purvis said to the squad. "But I want reports mailed whenever and wherever you can find a mailbox in those Godforsaken Cookson Hills. Do any of you have guns? "

"No, sir," Cecil said.

This obedience softened Purvis' face.

Honey choked back a chuckle.

"That's right," Purvis said. "No guns are authorized for this squad. I'm sending you in as scouts. Just find Floyd. We'll team up with the sheriffs to make the arrest."

Some agents shook their heads or looked away. Honey's eyes sparked mischief.

Lee knew Purvis had ignored the guns when the agents had raided the hideout.

"Now our three shooters at the Massacre are formally identified," Purvis went on. "Pretty Boy Floyd, Verne Miller and this Adam Richetti. That's official, from the Director."

"How would he know?" Honey said, Texas-style. "He wasn't there."

"Excuse me?" Purvis said.

"There you go with that official Washington voice," Honey smiled.

"Let's try to be a bit professional here," Purvis said.

"Oh, that word," Honey said.

"Whatever it may mean," Cecil added.

"Some of these identifications were developed through confidential sources," Purvis answered. "I think that's the best way to leave it for now."

The door opened. Special Agent Frank Smith entered, carrying a paper bag.

"Afternoon, everybody. I got some java and doughnuts here for the gang."

"Doughnuts!" Homer Bisbee sang out.

"Doughnuts! Doughnuts!" Honey yodeled.

"Aw, come on, fellas," Smith said. "Everyone likes doughnuts."

"Smith," Cecil said. "Haven't you heard? Real cops don't eat doughnuts."

"Y'see, in Chicago, sometimes we sit in the office all day," Honey explained. "There are no cases taking us outside. All we do is chow doughnuts and slurp coffee."

"Sometimes, that's all you're supposed to do," Homer Bisbee said.

"Cop humor," Honey said to Lee. "Relaxes the boys to laugh about something, even if it's silly."

"It's silly, all right," Lee said.

In the mirror, he saw how different he looked from the other agents. Nerves were pushing color into his cheeks. As a kid, fear had jangled him like this.

They waited until Purvis chose his doughnut. Then Smith passed out the steaming paper cups. Coffee fragrance filled the room.

"This came in yesterday," Smith said, taking out an oilskin envelope and handing it to Purvis. "The police passed it to us to dust for prints."

Purvis set down his coffee on the bedside table and squinted at the envelope, then shook it until a plain postcard tumbled out.

It was addressed to the Kansas City Police, Kansas City, Missouri.

With a tip of his pen, Purvis flipped the card over. A message was printed in pencil.

DEAR SIR:

I CHARLES FLOYD WANT IT MADE
KNOWN THAT I DID NOT
PARTICIPATE IN THE MASSACRE
OF OFFICERS AT KANSAS CITY

CHARLES FLOYD

Purvis stared at the card. The others crowded around.

"This is the best proof we've gotten so far that Floyd did the killings," Purvis' voice climbed. "How could he do a thing this stupid? Send us a postcard?"

"How could he do any of these things?" Honey sipped. "How could he kill four cops to free one lousy con? How could Floyd be Floyd?"

"Today must be letter day," Homer Bisbee said. "Floyd and the Director."

"Smith, you brought in the letter with our coffee?" Cecil said. "What if they had gotten switched?"

"You've got to remember," Hollis said. "These killers are another breed. They're not like us. As Honey says, Floyd is Floyd."

Cecil gestured with his paper cup. "Have any of you seen the papers this morning? People are howling mad about this Massacre. Read them, you'll see."

"We've got dozens of statements from witnesses in that station," Purvis said. "It seems like the whole country was in the Union Station yesterday morning."

"In a sense, they all were," Cecil said. "Everyone had a front row seat. And they did not like it. Up until now, crooks have seemed like good old boys who could take your mind off hard times. That's all changed since yesterday. Now everyone knows that they will butcher daddies and husbands for a favor."

"That's enough coffee and pep talk," Honey said, glancing at Lee and Cecil. "The three of us are hunting Floyd?"

"We're hunting Floyd!" Lee and Cecil chorused.

"And," Honey said, "We're going to put him in a box."

CHAPTER 17: Summer, 1933

COOKSON HILLS, OKLAHOMA

In the Choctaw Indian language, "Oklahoma" meant "The Land of the Red People."

To Lee, Oklahoma meant being afraid. His fear began as soon as they entered the Cookson Hills, one of the wildest places in the country. No paved roads cut through the Hills. Ridge after ridge folded them in deeper and deeper. The locals roistered without telephones, electricity or laws. Jesse James had hidden out here. Now rumors flowered that Floyd had gone to ground somewhere in the Hill country.

They stripped off their Bureau regulation clothes and dressed in cotton and canvas work clothes with floppy hats.

Honey, Cecil and Lee checked ghost towns like Toomer and Split Pine and Muskrat where empty cabins creaked at their footsteps.

Lee clutched his sawed-off .45. He smelled the dust from the cabins, mixed with the smell of stagnant water from nearby swamps. A burnt taste of being scared hung in his mouth. His fair face kept flushing red from nerves.

Down one winding dirt road and up another, Cecil read through their notes while Lee drove.

"Washington says that Floyd stands 6'1", 240 pounds. Filled with corn dogs and home-brew suds. black hair and blue-gray eyes. Parts his hair in the middle. Slicks it down with grease. Just like the peckerwood that he is. Ruddy complexion with a small mouth and a large nose that I would like to shoot off."

Cecil looked away from notes. "You know what the French say. '*Cherchez la femme*. Find the woman'."

"He had been married, more or less," said Honey, "to Ruby Leonard Hargraves."

Cecil held up the notes.

"Sixteen at the blessed event," smiled Honey. "Ruby, the fair virgin, five-foot six, with auburn hair and brown eyes."

Cecil nodded.

"She and Pretty Boy have an eight-year-old son, Jack Dempsey Floyd," Cecil said.

"Gonna be tough," observed Honey. "People here love him. The local boy who made good. Gives away stolen cash to these Okies. Visits his old mama whenever she sends for him. Hell, he's country. The people here have a family tradition of hating cops."

"I got something for his ass." Honey took out a gray canvas bag, stenciled PROPERTY OF THE TEXAS DEPARTMENT OF PUBLIC SAFETY from under Lee's feet.

He removed a chunky Thompson submachine gun. Even without the stock attached, the gun was as long as Lee's arm from shoulder to finger. The finned barrel smelled of gun oil.

"Is that authorized?" Lee joked.

"Ask me how much I care."

"I never saw one before," Lee said. "At New Agents' Training in Washington, they just showed us pistols. They said that if we behaved, someday Congress might arm us."

"When a monkey sandpapers himself," Honey said.

Lee hefted the gun as they bounced out of town It was like holding a fat baby. Each thick round drum held fifty slugs.

"Plus, Cecil and I bought two shotguns in KC," Honey said, "and we sawed them down nice and short. They're in the trunk. This evening, we'll stop and give you a little target practice."

•

They stopped and made camp for the night.

Cecil built a fire from fallen branches and set to work cooking bacon, beans and coffee.

Honey taught Lee how to aim and fire the .45 revolver two-handed. The heavy gun bucked, but Lee managed to put some slugs into a dead tree trunk.

"Wrap both hands around the gun," he said. "Point it like you point your finger. Up close, don't aim. Follow your eyes with your shots. Bend your knees for the kick. Makes you a smaller target. That's your combat crouch. Instinctive shooting."

The two shotguns felt easier for Lee. He had been hunting with shotguns since the sixth grade.

"Remember, you always have to aim a shotgun," Honey said. "Especially a sawed-off like this. Use these sawed-offs for close range against a man-sized target. Snap it in tight against your hips there."

Cecil banged on a tin plate with a large spoon.

"Unfortunately, no doughnuts will be served with tonight's repast."

"Don't you know about Purvis's sweet tooth?" Honey asked as Cecil slapped beans onto Lee's plate. "Why, he just flat-out loves doughnuts. That boot-licker Homer Bisbee is always bringing him coffee and doughnuts."

"Homer Bisbee sits and has a cup with McQueeny, every chance he gets," Cecil said. "Neither of them are cops. They're office people. In Yiddish they'd be called *kirchof gemussen*. That means 'cemetery vegetables'. Types who want to work, live and die at their desks. Coffee and doughnuts. They think that we are jerks to take chances out in the streets."

"Maybe they right," Honey grunted.

A hound dog came out of the woods and approached their camp fire. His gray coat was mangy and caked blood was oozing from one paw. Honey fretted and scanned him for signs of rabies.

"Hi, nice puppy," Cecil purred. "Nice boy, nice puppy. Want some dinner? "

"Cecil, you're nuts. That thing ain't coming near me. I'll blow his filthy head off."

"Nice puppy. Honey, I was hoping to get a dog out of this road trip deal. You two can get kind of dull."

Cecil threw a hunk of bacon fat over the hound dog's head.

The dog saw it, scooped it up and ran into the dark woods.

•

After chow, they sat around the fire until it turned into a hump of red coals. Lee heard owls hooting and the sudden rush of their wings.

Honey opened a glass jar of moonshine. The campsite filled with the reek of raw liquor.

"We've got agents looking for Floyd everywhere," Honey said. "We just happen to be the ones doing the road trip here. Running through these hills seems stupid, but it's got to be done. The country's too small for Floyd. It used to be that he could hide in these Cooksons forever. But now we're going to nail the fat son of a bitch."

"Go to sleep," Cecil said.

Honey took a long sip.

"Ah, wonderful," Honey said. "Either of you want a taste?"

"No, thanks," Lee said.

"He don't approve, Cecil, I can tell," Honey said. "That's okay. You get to sleep your way and I'll get to sleep mine."

"He could be circling our camp right now," Cecil said. "Biding his time to ambush us."

Lee gulped in some air.

"Cecil, are you trying to scare me?" Honey asked.

"Waiting, out there. Pulling back the bolt on his own Tommy gun. Sighting in on your spongy gut. Killing law-dogs who track him is his only way to get clear. Floyd's desperate now."

Lee rubbed his fingertips across the .45's battered rubber grips. His eyes danced from shape to shape among the solemn trees.

"Ambush by night has your throat cut before you wake up," Cecil said. Lee could not tell if he was serious or not. "These hills make it easy for him."

Lee smelled the wood smoke and his own sweat as he tried to relax himself to sleep.

"Can't get to sleep, youngster?" Cecil asked.

Lee's jaw snapped.

"Maybe you should try counting Public Enemies," Cecil said. "Instead of sheep."

Lee heard something else scrape a branch in the woods close by. His hand snaked out for the .45 again.

"Whoa, there, youngster," Cecil said. "Or else, you'll blast Honey or myself if we arise in the night to answer nature."

"When we wring out the sponge," Honey said.

"That noise is nothing that will hurt you," Cecil said. "That's just a 'haint'. Some poor dead creature haintin' these woods before its soul can rest."

"Or, that noise is a 'hide-behind'," Honey said. "You hear the noise, look up fast, but the 'hide-behind varmint' is so fast that he can hide-behind anything before you can see him."

Something choked out of Lee's mouth, half-gasp and half-giggle.

"Haints and hide-behinds," Honey drawled. "The dreaded."

Lee inched himself closer to their car. If anyone attacked them, he was driving away first, he told himself. Cecil and Honey would not need his help, not with all their experience.

Honey wrapped himself in a blanket, rolled over and soon was snoring through his broken nose. Cecil quieted soon after.

Only Lee lay awake, his eyes making murderous shapes out of the dark shrubs and tree trunks. He kept his glasses folded in a case next to him. His fingertips brushed the chunky .45 by his side.

Lee shivered as the owls kept hooting. He wished he were home with his family.

Lee recalled going home to Nebraska from Chicago for Christmas the year before. The past ten months felt like a lifetime now.

●

Light snow had covered the Midwest.

Everyone grumbled about President Roosevelt, feeling that the rich playboy with his cigarette holder had better change things in a hurry.

Lee's family was trying to live without any frills. Nearby farms were going under, seized by the banks.

Lee had put on his old clothes and had slept deep and well in the family farmhouse.

The day after Christmas, he went walking over the farm property. Steak, potatoes and pumpkin pie from dinner still weighted him down. The light snow swirled around him. His boots crunched over the roads.

He left the Childress property and cut across different spreads. The farmers used to chase him and his pals off these fields but nobody cared anymore. Harvest time had come and gone, without much work done.

The fields of buffalo grass lay fallow. Their tops poked out through the snow. Nothing moved, nothing worked, nothing grew. The bread basket was ripped empty.

Lee walked down to the Shad Road where he used to deliver papers on his bike. He crossed the little wooden bridge and went down to the creek where he used to hide things. He hunkered down in the frosty notch and watched the creek trickle past. The water looked brown and icy, moving over the wet black rocks, gurgling. He thought about the Bureau and his furnished room in Chicago.

When he clambered back up to the bridge, the snow had started falling again. The flakes swirled around him, lighting on the ground and sticking to the buffalo grass. He pulled the mackinaw closer around himself and began making his way home.

CHAPTER 18: Summer, 1933

COOKSON HILLS, OKLAHOMA

They drove through the town of Sallisaw at dawn and hid their car in the woods. The weather felt damp around them. Clumps of fog still hung in the hollows.

Lee's color climbed as they crept up on the Floyd family farm, three miles outside of Tahlequah.

The agents crept like Indians, from tree to tree. The night-time animals were bedding down for the day. Deer-hooves drummed against the leafy ground.

They saw no sign of Pretty Boy or anyone else in the flat brown house with three broken windows in front. The front door sagged on hinges. Firewood humped on the porch.

About a hundred feet from the house, Honey fashioned a watching spot from the thick brush. The trio squatted down in the piled branches and waited.

"Bureau trains us to be patient," Honey whispered.

"It doesn't train us to be stupid," Cecil said in a normal tone.

Honey made a face like he was throwing up.

"Jesus wept, Cecil," he hissed. "Keep it down. These are poor white trash hunting fools with hounds of hell to match. Maybe they mate with them. They got the same sharp hearing, anyway. You want the whole hairy, sweaty clan down on us?"

"That does paint a picture," Lee whispered.

"Don't you start, too, College Flapper," Honey said. "There's no other way to hunt this skunk."

Lee could not move his eyes from the farmhouse. He jammed his hands in his pockets so nobody could see them shake.

"Do you really think that Pretty Boy Floyd is in that house?" Lee stammered.

"Do you want me to ask?"

"All my joints ache," Lee said. "This woodcraft sneaking skulking around is not for me."

"Brother Yalie," Honey hissed. "Did young Childress say 'skulking?'"

"Indeed, he did, Brother Ross," Cecil said.

"And do skulking mean what I think it do?"

"It do."

They kept watching and munched pork sandwiches. The hours dragged into afternoon and evening.

"How did Floyd get that moniker, 'Pretty Boy'?" Lee asked. "He isn't that pretty."

"An Iowa railroad cop named Purcell gave me the story," Honey said. "Seems Floyd was buying some poontang in a cat house. And the boss bitch gave him a free one, saying 'I want you for myself, Pretty Boy.' Probably gave him a dose."

"We're never going to find him," Lee said.

"Kid, you're sounding like a man looking to quit the Bureau," Honey said. "We'll find him. And the Bureau will fix this country's crime problem."

"Sure. All 266 of us."

Lee's stomach turned over. He was still afraid.

"I don't belong here," Lee said.

"Never said you did," Honey muttered.

"This is for tough guys. The toughest thing I ever did was go eight rounds with a mean welterweight named Rinfret. I mean, we were both lawyers, for God's sake."

"That's all for now," Honey said. "Let's git before someone notices our car. Pick this up later, after dark."

Driving, they bumped over the mud lanes that headed into town. There was still some daylight left.

A young Okie kid started running down the lane as they passed, dogs yapping after him.

"There goes trouble," Honey observed.

"Folks are going to notice us," Lee said. "We can come back tomorrow."

"We can't stay here on this road, that's a pipe cinch." Cecil said.

"Naw. The folks'll recognize us for laws and start a-chunking things at us." Honey had great faith in country folks' feeling for strangers.

He slid the canvas bag under his arm.

"I reckon we moved that car enough," Honey said. "Let's head back to Floyd's house and take a new position to watch for him, If we see him, we take him."

"By ourselves?" Lee's face twisted. "What about the local sheriff, for back-up?"

"Are you nuts, kid? You'll get us killed graveyard dead. What about Kansas City? Remember that the city cops leaked word to Floyd? Can't trust nobody."

"I'll drive into town like we was lost and head back towards Floyd's place," Cecil said.

He turned the car.

The windshield exploded.

"Oh, no!" Lee yelped.

"Outta the car!" Honey shouted. "Get cover. Stay here, you dead!"

Guns flashed all around them. Slugs smacked into the Ford.

"Move out, Lee!" Cecil shouted.

Outside the car, Honey squatted down. He could see Okies standing on their front porches, all along the street. Guns boomed off each porch. The kid who had run to warn the Okies was firing, too, steadying a long goose gun with a stringy forearm.

"This is the voice of the people!" Cecil shouted. "Just like Lexington and Concord."

There was a grove of trees next to the Ford. Lee ran into the grove and hid. He could not find his .45. All he had was his credentials case from the trunk. He stepped back out of the grove and waved the black leather case open, like a young preacher waving the Bible.

"Hold your fire!" he screamed. "We're government agents!"

"They know that, stupid!" Cecil said. "That just makes it worse."

He cooly rammed stubby shotgun shells into his bib overalls' pockets.

"Stay down, lawyer. Ready, Honey?"

Honey rolled up and ripped off a burst from the Tommy gun. The Okies stopped shooting.

Cecil crept closer to the nearest gunners on the porch.

The Okies started to step back off their porches and back into their houses. Honey put another burst high above their heads and flanked Cecil.

"Top windows" Cecil shouted. He threw himself sideways and triggered off a shotgun blast from his sawed-off.

Another Tommy opened up from the house. Lee watched a line of shots stitch up the dirt. The Ford sagged. Honey fired back.

"We're cooked!" Lee said. "We're gonna wind up like Caffrey!"

"Caffrey!" Honey shouted it like a war cry.

He tucked the Tommy in, rolled to a boulder and was up on a knee when the house door opened.

Someone came out. Honey and Cecil fired.

Windows went out. Woodchips flew.

Floyd, a big bearish man in overalls, stepped back inside the house, his Tommy chattering.

Lee jumped into the car's back seat and hoisted the shotgun out.

Floyd came back out the door. He pinned them down with his Tommy gun.

Lee fired one, two, three buckshot loads at him.

Floyd staggered. Denim snips flew.

Honey was on his feet now, moving fast.

Floyd kneeled, reaching for the Tommy. His fingers brushed it. Cecil brought his shotgun on target.

"We got him!" Lee shouted. "We got him!"

A volley of shots ripped through the field. Turning, Lee saw the Okies were leaving their porches and coming closer to the agents. They fired as they approached.

Cecil spun and went down, the sawed-off flying away. Honey threw himself behind a stump.

Floyd burst out of the house, blood on his denims, the Tommy held in one hand. He fired as he ran.

Lee reloaded in time to send two loads whistling past him. The locals kept up their fire. Their slugs hit the trees next to Honey.

Floyd ran straight to the next house, some fifty feet away. Trees covered him and he was already out of range.

Lee reloaded furiously. He could see Floyd's overalls through the dark green trees. Then in shadow. Then gone.

The Okies stopped firing. They started melting back to their homes. Lee saw that Honey had dragged Cecil back behind the car, covering his body with his own.

He lay like that, exhausted.

"Where you hit, Cecil?"

"Forearm. It bounced off the shotgun, isn't bad."

"He's going! He's getting away!" Lee said.

"He's already gone, kid. You can't take on the whole town."

"They helped him. They took him away from us! That wasn't even Floyd's house!"

"Well," Honey said. "Maybe he was visiting folks."

"He IS a sociable type," Cecil said.

"Lee," Honey said. "Bring the car around so's I can load the Yalie in. Don't worry. The Okies ain't shooting. They got what they want."

Lee ran to the car and tried to start it up. He switched on the headlights and turned them onto the woods behind the Okies' houses.

He knew Floyd was in there, wounded, hit more than once, panting like an animal.

The citizens were back inside their houses, their lights out, watching the agents, possum guns in their hands.

The car would not start.

"Engine dead," Lee said.

Honey propped Cecil up against a tree. The rented Ford's windows were smashed, the tires blown out, with glass all over the seats.

Lee finally found his .45 on the car floor. It had probably fallen out of his belt when he jumped out of the car. He did not want the others to know he had dropped it.

"We almost had him," Lee panted. "Those Okies must hate the government."

"You might say that," Cecil answered. "You see, he's one of them."

"That's enough sociology," Honey snapped. "Lee, take the shotguns. We're gonna have to walk out of town and leave the car here. Make sure you got your creds. They'll torch this car tonight, that's for sure."

It was dark along the road. The three men walked back the way they had come, the guns hidden in their bags.

"If we see anyone on the road, what'll you tell them?" Lee asked.

"I'll tell them the truth," Honey said. "We've been hunting and we had an accident."

CHAPTER 19: Summer, 1933

CHICAGO, ILLINOIS

"After something like that, you could stand a taste," Honey said.

It was four days after the shootout.

Leaving Floyd's town, they had walked for hours until a liquored-up farmer gave them a ride to the next post office. Honey had woken up the postmaster, identified themselves and borrowed a car to get to a train station. Conductors saw their creds and let them ride for free into Chicago.

Lee worried that they would slam him for not getting Floyd. They said nothing about it. That worried him more.

The Alexian Brothers Hospital treated Cecil's forearm wound and sent him home.

Purvis read their reports. He seemed to care more about the ruined car.

"The Director says, and I agree, that we can't take immediate action against that town," Purvis said. "It'll just stir things up and make Floyd harder to catch. Smart thing is to do nothing. You're sure that it was Floyd?"

"Dead sure," Honey said. "He might have been using another house as a hideout. Smart fella. He's gone from there by now."

Honey and Lee were driving around Chicago in a new rented car.

Cecil was home, with his six different breeds of dogs lying quietly near their master's bed.

Cecil's tall blonde wife Becky tended him while he played with his puppies. Becky wore her hair cut short like a dancing girl in the movies, with pure white teeth set in her lean face.

"It's just a nick," Cecil reassured them. "We were lucky. All we lost was our car and our clothes."

"And Floyd," Honey said.

•

Lee pulled the car over at 63rd Street and South Halstead and set the handbrake.

He was still shaky. He figured he would sit down with Honey and talk about resigning from the Bureau. He didn't want any more gun battles. The Depression would end someday and he wanted to still be alive.

Honey took out a briefcase from the back seat. They left the car and walked through a thick, steel-rimmed door marked "Borden & Pine – We Aim To Please."

The joint was a big place with high ceilings and tables with red checkered tablecloths and candles in bowls. It was already dark, in late afternoon. A pool table invited them. A group of hard guys dressed in sleek dark suits and silk neckties, wearing gold jewelry at their wrists and throats, were drinking noisily around the pool table. Some glittery girls were moving around them, laughing at what they said.

A tough-looking Italian waiter in a gold hip-length jacket got up from his coffee cup when they walked in.

"Can I help you gents?" he asked.

"Vote out Prohibition."

"We're having a private birthday party here, bub," the waiter said. "The tables are all taken."

Honey grinned. "No problem, partner. Sammy knows me. So does Peanuts. My name's Ross. Me and Junior here aim to drink up and relax some. No trouble."

"You're sure Peanuts knows you?"

"Knows me good."

"That's okay." He moved aside."Take a table."

A blonde waitress with smoky greenish eyes in a clinging black dress came over to Lee and Honey as they both ordered bootleg Canuck rye. They watched her move away, back in the world of women again.

When they had tossed down the first round, the waitress leaned close to Honey.

"Don't mind the party over there," she said. "Peanuts' kid had his first birthday today and Peanuts is feeling pretty good."

"You tell Peanuts congratulations from us. And bring us another round, with beer chasers, sweetheart."

Lee unsnapped the briefcase. He took out a sheaf of Bureau forms and began writing up their report.

"By God, kid, I feel good," Honey said.

For the first time in weeks, they wore clean clothes. Lee drank and scrutinized the waitress.

"Nice," Honey said. "Very, very nice."

He bottomed his glass and turned to Lee."I'm not sure if this federal service is gonna bring out the finest qualities in you. You may not be able to go home and live with the folks afterwards."

"What are you talking about?"

Lee slid the report across to Honey.

Honey took out a thick Parker pen and scratched his signature on the top sheet.

A glittery girl from the birthday party walked past. She had dark shining hair, pulled back over one bare shoulder.

"Good evening, gentlemen," she said, tugging at her red dress.

Honey grinned back as he watched her sway away.

They ordered rich food for the first time in weeks – prime ribs of beef *au jus*, whipped potatoes, and creamed spinach. They kept on drinking and feeling good as they argued over the final report.

"Cecil got hit by stray fire," Honey said. "We'll put down that the townspeople opened up on us. We think we saw Floyd, but we had no weapons, and we fired no shots. The good citizens thought we were revenuers, so they blasted our car. That's all she wrote."

"If we tell the truth, maybe we can push the Bureau into authorizing pieces for us," Lee said.

"And maybe we can push them into keeping us in the office."

"If we had better guns and training, we could take on guys like Floyd and win."

"This ain't the way," said Honey, his drawl coming out stronger with the rye. "Can't tell them we broke the law, and then ask them to change it."

"Nobody, but nobody, in this outfit ever tells the truth," sighed Lee.

"Who wants to hear it? They don't wanna know. Oh, Jesus, Mister Hoover, why did you do this to me? Lawyers and accountants. Jesus, Childress, this is just your first taste of the world. I don't know why I bother."

Lee dropped his chin, a boxing reflex. He got up to walk off his anger and found himself at the pool table. The girl in the red dress sidled up to him.

"D'you know how to play?" he asked.

She turned her cool eyes fully on him.

"I'm a champ," she said.

"Let's see."

Honey passed by and looked at her playing alongside Lee. He nodded to himself and went upstairs to the other girls.

The whiskey gave Lee courage. Usually he was shy around girls. He racked the balls and broke them with a clean shot, going after the high balls.

"I'm Billie," said the girl. "What's your name, sweetie, and where did you learn to play pool so nice and all? "

"College. There was nothing else to do in the winter."

"I'm from a hick town up near the reservation in Michigan." She spoke directly, looking into his eyes. Her looks warmed him, like the whiskey. "I'm a Menominee Indian. See? Firewater. But I've been civilized, so I drink martinis."

She took the stick in her slim fingers, leaning her full, ripe body down low. Her black hair touched the green felt.

The man called Peanuts came through the room. He was a tall and elegant man who looked like a Roman senator. He carried a tray filled with drinks. His every move showed discipline.

His pals watched him approach Lee.

"Private party, kid," Peanuts said.

"Who're you?" Lee asked. Drinking made him reckless.

"San-ny Claus," he growled. "With the hooch for presents. You with Honey?"

"I'm with Honey," Lee mumbled.

Peanuts eyed him up and down

"Okay, then," Peanuts said.

He passed out glasses.

"Ey, there you go, kids. Gin martini for you, Billie. And you're sticking with rye, pal? The drinks're on me. Today's my kid's birthday so everyone drinks up."

"You're a sport, Peanuts." Billie's hand brushed against Lee. "Here's to the kid."

"Here's to him."

Lee's rye burned nicely.

She eased herself over the table and lined up a shot, the four into to the far left hand pocket.

The ball bounced around the rim of the pocket. It settled against the bumper.

"Ay!" Billie cried.

Lee turned and looked her over, drunkenly. She looked good to him. Now he could see she looked like an Indian, with her glossy black hair and dark eyes.

The cue ball was surrounded by solids. He tapped the twelve with the cue ball to avoid a foul and placed the stick in Billie's hands. He adjusted her fingers. A perfume he didn't recognize wafted from her. It smelled expensive.

"Hold the stick this way," Lee said.

"You a pool hustler for a living?" she asked.

Lee shook his head.

"Then what?"

"I'm a lawyer." He looked for Honey, but Honey was gone. "Just barely getting by."

As she turned back to the table, her breast brushed against him again. Her body moved gently under the dress as she lined up the shot.

"Ay!" Billie yelled again as the four ball refused to drop into the pocket.

Lee spent the rest of the night trying to get sober and trying to hold on to his stomach.

Home was a cab ride to Billie's apartment on the North Side.

She shucked off her dress to show him her body.

She held him as he glided down on top of her, her dark eyes secret and catlike.

Afterward, Lee slept.

Then he was running cold water in her sink, trying not to get sick. Trying to stand straight and ignore the rye still in him. He would never know how much money he had spent. She could have rifled through his pockets to take money or read his credentials.

She put him out later. He wanted her again and again.

But she did not want him.

CHAPTER 20: August 18, 1933

CHICAGO, ILLINOIS

At just past nine, Lee entered an office on South Halstead marked 'Dr. Nathan Picker, MD.' A pale frail man with mud-colored hair and restless brown eyes slouched behind a flat gray tin desk and coughed in Lee's direction. He coughed like a smoker.

"Help you, son?" he asked in a Midwest drawl.

"Like to see the doctor," Lee stammered. "Can't sleep. Got nightmares. Gotta job where I worry about dying."

The man looked at him.

"Everyone worries about dying," the man said.

"Doctor coming in?" Lee asked.

"I'm the doctor. Nat Picker. My patients sometimes call me 'Nit-picker.'"

"Lost my appetite," Lee said. "Just wanna stay in bed all day."

"You look a little crude," Dr. Picker said.

"Got drunk last night," Lee said. "Still feel crummy as we speak."

"Part of the pattern," Dr. Picker said. "Five dollars, basic exam. You got it? Come into the exam room. Take off your shirt."

He probed Lee, took blood pressure, peered into his eyes with a pencil flash, palped his arms.

To Lee, it took too long.

At last Dr. Picker finished with his tests, and they sat, facing each other.

"Your vitals are a mess, son," Dr. Picker said. "Probably holding onto your job too hard. What's your trade?"

Lee did not want a record of this visit anywhere. Everyone served at the pleasure of Director Hoover. Nobody would ever admit to having stress problems. The Bureau could bounce him back onto the cold Omaha streets for no reason at all. He thought hard. The doctor waited.

"Auto sales," Lee said.

"From Chicago, son?"

"Omaha."

"Your folks gotta home there?'

"Dad has a farm."

"Go back to it," he said. "Forget auto sales. Help your folks. Eat and sleep regular. Stay on like this, you're gonna have real serious problems soon. I see what some call a nervous breakdown coming your way."

"I can't quit my job."

"You better," Dr. Picker said. "Go home."

At noon, Lee was back in the field office with a killer hangover that stayed with him. His head felt cottony. He craved cold ice cream. He signed in and found McQueeny dozing in the bullpen over some reports.

Lee nudged him awake.

"Good morning, young Childress," McQueeny said. He, settled back in his chair and used his usual tone of voice. He always spoke low, like there were people eavesdropping. "While you were gone, we've been busy. There's a slew of bank robberies by some new talent. Ever heard of a party named Dillinger? John Dillinger? "

"Not a whisper."

"Young Dillinger is an up-and-coming bad apple. If you still lived in Indiana, you'd know the name. Chicago hasn't heard about him yet. Hoosier people are talking about him, and the Indiana newspapers are calling for his arrest.

"But one thing's strange. This Dillinger fellow is nothing. He's not a killer, like Verne Miller, or this fella Floyd that we are chasing. But for some reason, people pay attention to him. He runs a gang of slobs called 'The White Caps.' They wear white caps all the time so everyone knows them. These are not slick desperadoes, son. These are fellas who could screw up a cheese sandwich."

"Don't tell me," said Lee. "The Bureau wants us to go after these clowns."

"Monitor. Just monitor them. Both Purvis and Hoover need to make a big splash. They live or die on publicity. There is talk that Washington may phase the Bureau out. We'll all be out of work.

"But if the Bureau can show that Dillinger is a menace to the American way of life, and we can nail him in a spectacular way, the public will love us."

"Is that all we care about, the public and the politicians?" Lee asked. The hangover rasped his voice. "What about real work?"

"Dillinger is real work. He should be in jail. And maybe we'll put him there."

"It seems like all we care about is public opinion."

"We should care. Without public support, we're dead in the water," McQueeny said. "What's the matter, young Childress? Having second thoughts about crime-crushing in the Bureau?"

"I don't see much crime-crushing."

"We're doing what we can. All that Washington and the people will tolerate. Aren't you happy here?"

"Doing what? I'm just sitting out the Depression. There are times I'd rather be in a law office drawing up wills. That's what I went to school for."

"Then you should think about resigning. People will always need lawyers, even in the Depression."

"Meanwhile," Lee said bitterly, "we can't look for real killers like Floyd. That doesn't make sense. We should put every agent on Floyd. He's killed four cops."

"Dillinger has some killers with him, too. One is a small-time Chicago hood named Lester Gillis. He also uses the name George Nelson. The newspapers call him Baby Face Nelson. He's a little screwy. He likes to pull those triggers. He escaped from Joliet prison. Now he's in Chicago, robbing banks. So we want both Nelson and Dillinger. If we can get them on a federal crime and roll them both up, we'll get the power, guns, funding, and most important, the respect we don't get now."

"What about the Floyd case?"

"By God, you are stubborn. Floyd'll lie low. But Dillinger will make the news."

"So we'll have to make Dillinger look dangerous."

"Naturally," McQueeny nodded. "That's politics."

Lee glanced around the bullpen, wondering where Honey was. Usually he was one of the first agents in the office each morning.

Homer Bisbee came inside the bullpen, walking pigeon-toed as always and carrying coffee and doughnuts. His thick black hair was combed with water, and his beer stomach was jammed into a vest.

The bullpen telephone rang. Homer Bisbee snagged it.

"Bureau of Investigation, Homer Bisbee speaking . . . Yes, Inspector . . . No, I never had any car accident. Of course, I'm sure. Hello, hello, inspector? Can you hear me?"

"This is one of Honey's tricks," McQueeny whispered to Lee. "Call up one of us and sweat him about denting an official car signed out to that agent. Then Honey hangs up."

Homer Bisbee's moustache started twitching.

"Fellas, that was an Inspector from Washington claiming I damaged a car."

"Oh, yes," McQueeny joshed him, deadpan. "I heard about that."

Lee felt relieved that Honey was all right this morning, after the previous wild night.

●

John Dillinger, built square and chunky, dressed in flashy suits. His parents were French-Americans who had settled in a Quaker hamlet outside Indianapolis. The locals called Indianapolis 'India-no-place' and Dillinger solved the boredom problem as a teenager by stealing chickens and robbing a local grocer.

He scored nine years in prison for his first job. Inside, he learned how to pull professional bank jobs and started putting a gang of his own together. When he got out, his White Cap gang hit gas stations and stores all over Indiana.

On Father's Day, 1933, the day after the Kansas City Massacre, Dillinger accompanied his father to the local Friends Meeting Church. He had never visited the church before, even as a boy.

The lady grocer in the pulpit preached a sermon on the prodigal father and the prodigal son. Tears rolled down Johnny's face, streaking his prison-pale cheeks. He patted his father's hand, like someone at a funeral.

It *was* a funeral.

The honest and law-abiding Johnny Dillinger was dead and nobody would ever see him again.

After the service, he chatted with the Quakers and held the preacher by the hand.

"You'll never know how much good that sermon has done me," Dillinger said.

Everyone smiled.

They wanted to see him get a break now, in the era of the New Deal.

•

The day after the sermon, the White Caps hit places in Fort Wayne, Muncie, and East Chicago. Dillinger shot his way out of a police trap and fled across the state line to Kentucky, where he did some bank jobs.

In July, he came back to Indianapolis to visit his sister, Aubrey, at her farm. Two constables were looking for him, and they staked out Aubrey's farmhouse while Dillinger was out joy-riding with her. When he came back, the cops were snoozing in their patrol car, so they missed him as he came in the driveway.

Dillinger hid in the apple orchard with a pistol as day stretched into an afternoon. He catnapped off and on as the breeze blew over his sister's unplowed fields.

He grinned about the banks. He was just doing what bankers and big companies did, taking risks and building capital. Nobody had gotten hurt.

He was dozing when the sound of a car engine woke him.

He slid the hammer back on the pistol.

A tan roadster turned onto the Dillinger driveway and stopped. A tall, thin, stranger in a city suit got out.

The stranger spoke with Dillinger's father, saying he was Ed Hollis from the Bureau of Investigation Chicago office. Dillinger's father just shrugged.

Hollis took a good look around the farm and then drove away.

Dillinger waited until the engine noise had died down. He left the orchard and cut across the neighboring fields to where he had hidden his car in the woods.

CHAPTER 21: Mid-November 1933

CHICAGO, ILLINOIS

Lee had slept lightly ever since Oklahoma. He and the other agents had been working so much since July they had missed the seasons changing. Files grew as new cases came in.

Late one night, there was a tap at his hotel room door.

Groggy, Lee opened it to let in Billie. She smelled richly of tobacco and whiskey.

They went to bed without talking much.

Afterward, they both slept, wrapped up in each other, exhausted.

When he woke up, she was gone. Nothing was touched. His gun and Bureau creds were where he had left them.

•

Billie came back a few nights later, and this time she stayed longer. They started off taking a bath in Lee's tub.

"Boy, you're something different from the men I usually see," Billie said between puffs on a cigarette. "And you're so young. You make me feel good, and you're too young to even know why."

She splashed some water onto his chest.

"How did you get past the desk clerk?" Lee asked.

"How did I get inside?" Her black eyebrows raised. "Lee, that's my business. It's no trick getting inside any Chicago hotel. Especially a cheap one like this. This dump is the bottom of the hotel barrel."

"Stay here a while longer."

"Maybe. We'll see."

Again, Lee woke up alone.

He raised the window a crack and listened to the early morning traffic along Oriental Avenue.

Then he dressed rapidly in a dark gray suit, white shirt, black knitted necktie, white handkerchief and black wing-tips.

He squinted at his face in the mirror. Billie was right when she said that even at 24, he still looked like a kid. But new lines scored under the eyes.

Lee put his black credentials folder into his right inside pocket as Honey had taught him. That way, when he reached in with his left hand to identify himself, his right hand was free to draw and fire.

On the radio, Will Rogers was talking about Prohibition being voted out. The noble experiment was ending as a failure.

"People are wondering why the cops can't catch Dillinger," said Rogers' crackly voice. "He keeps getting away, and he's starting to pick up big money from his crime spree."

•

Lee took the streetcar into the Loop and got off at Adams Street. It was frosty out, with snow clouds overhead.

Cecil was bringing in a hefty man in a tweed overcoat.

"Morning, Cecil," Lee said. "Who's your friend?"

"No friend," Cecil said. "Buster Grimes. White slaver from Cicero. Buster heard some talk about Floyd. And he's gonna tell us all about it. Right, Buster?"

"You said I could leave when I wanna," Buster said in a Midwest twang. "Call me a white slaver, I'm leaving now."

"No, you ain't," Cecil said.

Buster swung and hit Cecil in the mouth. Lee started for Buster. Cecil waved him back. Workers in the lobby stared.

"Federal officer," Cecil said. Blood smeared his lip. "Now you got me mad."

Cecil jabbed Buster three times to the head. Buster's hands went up. Cecil bulled inside his arms. Cecil hammered fists into the tweed coat. Buster choked and slugged him again. Cecil kept punching. His fists moved like pistons. Buster gasped and fell on Cecil's foot.

Lobby people clapped and cheered.

"Yeeow!" Cecil yelped in his Yankee accent. "You hurt my foot!"

Lee helped Cecil plant Buster in a lobby chair. Buster's gut heaved in and out. They brought Buster upstairs to the office.

Homer Bisbee watched from his desk. Suran stepped closer to watch.

Cecil limped.

"You hurt?" Lee asked.

"Buster fell on my ankle. Sprained, by the feel of it. Honey says that I should stop razzing you, kid. Maybe he's right. You're a worker. You're no McQueeny."

"You beat me up," Buster gasped.

"You wanted to throw hands at me. These days, I am easily irritated, I'm no great boxer but I know a hawk from a handsaw."

"Sweet job," Lee said.

"You're not the only one who boxed in college," Cecil said. "There are more things in alleys and cathouse fights, college boy, than are dreamt of in all your ring philosophy. Shakespeare says so. My ankle really hurts."

"You going on sick leave?" Lee asked.

"A real cop? Are you kidding me?" Cecil said. "Suran, take Buster and book him with Chicago cops. Citizens' arrest. No handcuffs needed. Simple assault. Cool him in a cell and I'll sign the paperwork and jaw with him tomorrow."

"That ain't fair!" Buster gasped. "You made me hit you."

"See you in court with that sparkling defense," Cecil said.

Suran led Buster away. Buster walked with difficulty.

"You shouldn't do this fighting stuff," Homer Bisbee said. "We're not supposed to. This guy could sue you for overstepping your authority."

"Don't listen to him, Lee." Cecil said, smirking. "Homer Bisbee's upset today. He's got his privates twisted about some new regulations Hoover just sent us from Washington."

"We can't smoke in public," Homer Bisbee said. "We can't wear a dress shirt unless it's white. Have to leave telephone numbers where we can be reached at all times, even going to the movies. Can't drink coffee while on duty or do anything that might embarrass the Bureau."

"And still no guns and no real arrest powers," Cecil said. "That's the real embarrassment. They want to turn us into office workers and not real cops. Ha! We'll show 'em! Don't take your coat off, Childress, We've got a deal cooking in Michigan. Buster messed up my schedule. The other guys are all going to stake out the train station. Floyd's supposed to be coming into town. Saddle up."

They went down to the garage where the other teams were heating up their cars. Hollis and Winstead, McQueeny and Honey, and all the others were racing the engines and checking the gas gauges. A Victrola played an Army bugle call.

They looked up to see Cecil on the walkway above them. He waved his snap-brim hat.

"Look at you!" Cecil croaked, limping. "Cops! Real cops! We'll show them in Washington we're real cops!"

The car engines roared. The music changed. The Victrola played a cavalry charge. The bugles swelled the garage.

"I want arrests from each one of you!" Cecil said, "Collar me a bad guy today! I want guns and subjects off the street today! Real arrests from real cops!"

"Nice boxing, Cecil!" Winstead shouted. "Everyone in the building talking about ya."

"Ain't no real boxers at Yale!" Honey shouted. "Just boxing students. When Yalies learn enough, they can try boxing us Texans!"

"Doughnuts! Doughnuts!" Hollis sang out.

"Arrests!" Cecil was raging. "Get me arrests! Let's show Mister and Missus America what their Bureau can really do! Arrests!"

•

Lee and Cecil drove over the flat snowy plains towards River Rouge, Michigan.

"Buster also told me Adam Richetti was never at the Massacre," Cecil said. "He said that SAC Vetterli was too rattled to know what he was seeing. Vetterli saw Verne Miller's coat draped over the passenger seat, and he thought it was a third gunman. It was just Verne Miller and Pretty Boy Floyd who did the shooting that day."

"Where was Richetti?"

"Richetti was too plastered from drinking beer to go on a gun job. He was sleeping it off in Miller's house on Edgevale Road."

"Why does the Bureau say Richetti was at the Massacre?"

"Because it had looked like he was there. Remember, we got his fingerprints off those beer bottles in Miller's joint. That puts Richetti there. And Vetterli is our only eye-witness to their getaway, after the shooting. The other wits saw the shooting but they ran for cover."

"I don't know which story to believe," Lee said. He shifted gears going up a long, flat hill. "Could an experienced agent make that kind of mistake?"

"Anyone could, under those conditions. Vetterli had just seen five men slaughtered all around him by automatic weapons, he was hit in the arm, knocked down, looking through a rear window about ten yards away while the car was moving fast. Nobody's perfect. Vetterli thought he saw a third man."

Wind sliced the roadster. Cecil pulled his camel hair coat tighter around him, closed his eyes and put his head against the window glass.

"Ho-ney," he said softly. "Ho-ney. I wonder what Honey's doing now."

"Cecil, you know my anniversary came and went already?" Lee said. "I've got a full year in the Bureau now."

"I can take a hint. What would you like for a present? Probably some other job, huh? Use me as a reference."

They rode along in silence for a while until Lee sighted the church steeple he was looking for. He took his first left after the church and followed it for about three miles. There was another car parked alongside the road.

Lee braked his car and they got out. A pear-shaped man in a wool mackinaw and hiking boots stretched his way out of the other car.

"Chuck Hammond," the man said. "Town marshal for River Rouge. You're the Justice men I spoke to?"

Hammond had a dead-white face with bloodshot, bulging eyes. He looked like the Depression had ripped everything from him. Lee saw that look often now.

"I'm Special Agent Cecil Laughlin. You spoke to me. Your directions were pretty good. Thanks for waiting around. This is Agent Lee Childress."

Hammond nodded towards Lee.

"What've you got?" said Cecil.

"This gentleman had hisself a little accident," Hammond said. "Has some burn marks on his body and some puncture wounds, so I figured it might be a gang job and I called you. Could be one of those Dillinger guys."

"Dillinger," Cecil sighed.

"If you'll take a few steps back this way, you'll trip over the gentleman. Right there, by the roadside."

The body was nude and pink and wrapped in blankets. The wrists and ankles were tied together, jackknifing the body painfully. The dead man's face had been punctured dozens of times with something small, like a penknife. The groin area was burned and blistered.

"Looks like a familiar fellow to me," Cecil yanked a handful of the dead man's hair out. "We'll know in a minute."

He took the fingerprint kit from their car and squatted down next to the body.

"Do you know him?" the marshal asked.

"We know most of the big shots," Lee said, sounding like a kid playing copper. "We've got our ways to identify them."

"I did all right to call you Justice G-men?"

"You did right. And we'll do right by you." Cecil said. He took fingerprints from the dead man's thumbs and started to match them against his file cards in the briefcase. He held the cards up to get a better angle.

Then he put them down, walked over and kicked the dead body in the head. The head snapped to one side.

"It's Verne Miller, Lee," Cecil kicked again. "Mister Kansas City Massacre himself. Marshal, we owe you one. You want to kick him yourself?"

"That's what you call 'doing right'?" the marshal asked.

"You may get a cash reward, Marshal. The hair is dyed red but the roots are dark blond. The prints match, too. Old Verne must have talked back to someone." Cecil smirked. "One down, Lee. Now we can go after Pretty Boy. I wonder what Honey will say when he hears this."

CHAPTER 22: Thursday, November 30, 1933

CHICAGO, ILLINOIS

Thanksgiving, 1933, was different for Lee from the year before. He stayed in Chicago, running down leads on Floyd and Dillinger. The agents celebrated Verne Miller's end with making Homer Bisbee buy them coffee and doughnuts for a party.

Then the Bureau went on the move.

"This is a Bureau special, gentlemen," Purvis said. "Special assignment straight from the Director. Full-court press. Anyone needing a vacation day has to see me first. Don't count on it. Tell your wives and children that they'll have to wait a while for that vacation."

Floyd's wife was touring the countryside with her nine-year-old son, Jack Dempsey Floyd. They were traveling with a carnival company, promoting a film called "Crime Doesn't Pay."

Homer Bisbee went along with the carnival undercover as a roustabout carnival, keeping both Floyds under surveillance and eating huge cups of popcorn and cones of cotton candy.

The agents kept combing frozen villages throughout the Midwest.

Farmers saw the criminals cutting across fields. Mousy librarians recognized them from post office flyers. Truck drivers helped them fix flats.

Each sighting rang Purvis's designer home telephone on Chicago's Gold Coast.

The weeks passed in a flurry of false sightings and long waits.

On Christmas day, Lee staked out a farmhouse with Honey and Hollis, waiting for Floyd. Honey's wife gave them bags of cooked turkey to chew on all day.

Hollis stared out the window, chain-smoking. His sharpshooter eyes lit on birds that flew around their car. Working too much paled his face.

"Sometimes wonder if this war on crime is ever gonna end," Hollis said. His Adam's Apple bobbed in his scrawny neck. His small ears waggled as he talked. Wind ruffled his dark hair, parted in the middle and showing a pink scalp underneath.

"You put in another request for the Los Angeles office?" Honey asked.

"Had to," Hollis said. "Purvis will deny it. As usual. My wife needs a warmer climate, her doctors keep telling us. Warm weather helps a nervous disorder like she got. Some days, she's helpless. You fellows know all about it. There's no secrets in this Bureau. Just like my family back in Des Moines."

"Hollis, ya got your lawyer's ticket, like Childress here," Honey said. "You don't need all this mess. Today you look like your tail is dragging."

"Seems like this war just goes on, days like today," Hollis said. "Nobody caring. We neglect our families, birthdays, kids' graduations and our own feeling good just to get these jokers. And then juries set them free. Or judges give them suspended sentences. I can't figure it out. Lie awake nights worrying. But I want my kids growing up in a cleaner America than what we got now."

Floyd never showed up.

Chapter 23: January – February 1934

EAST CHICAGO, INDIANA – Monday, January 15, 1934

1934 arrived with the days feeling cold and grim.

The Depression was still grinding people down and breaking their spirits. They hoped FDR's New Deal would work and put some food in their bellies.

Dillinger's gang hit the First National Bank & Trust on Chicago Avenue. A bank teller hit the silent alarm.

It rang in the police station and some stores nearby.

Cops lurched up from their breakfast tables and bellied out the doors.

Others fumbled from the station to the bank on foot. Some raced in their bouncing old family cars.

One cop, Hobart Wilgus, thought that the bank might be testing the alarm. He entered the bank with his gun holstered. That was the chief's standing rule. Nobody wanted to scare the customers.

Dillinger put his Tommy gun on Wilgus and grabbed the cop's pistol.

"You go out ahead of me, copper," Dillinger said. "They might as well shoot you as me. We love you guys anyway."

Dillinger stepped down the bank steps, pushing Wilgus ahead of him with the Tommy gun.

An off-duty cop named O'Malley saw them. He was passing by the bank. He recognized Dillinger from the papers. He yanked out his service gun from under his topcoat.

Dillinger leveled the Tommy gun.

"Don't be a sucker!" Dillinger shouted. "It ain't your dough!"

O'Malley aimed. He shot. Slugs hit Dillinger's chest. Dillinger staggered. Holes showed in Dillinger's bulletproof vest.

Dillinger blasted O'Malley with his Tommy gun. He kept firing. O'Malley spun around and dropped down. He still held the gun.

O'Malley's round face twisted as he died. His crest of dark hair, that he carefully combed every morning, lay gummed with bloody brain tissue.

The gang got away.

•

CHICAGO, ILLINOIS – January 25, 1934

That icy morning, Purvis came into the bullpen to announce that Dillinger had been arrested in Tucson, Arizona. The agents cheered and clapped.

That afternoon, they went back on the streets, looking for Floyd and Richetti.

They checked flophouses, pawnshops, bookie joints, cat houses and gin mills

They came up empty.

•

COOKSON HILLS, OKLAHOMA – February 15, 1934

Hoover finally pressured the Oklahoma governor to let the law clean up the Cookson hills.

Over 1,000 lawmen went openly into the Cooksons. Deputy sheriffs, town constables, and Osage tribal police joined the Feds, armed with deer rifles, coach gun shotguns and Henry carbines from the Civil War.

They covered more than ninety square miles, some on horseback and some on foot. They bagged just a few outlaws.

In Tulsa, after the raid, Lee overheard a deputy saying that someone in the governor's office had leaked word to the Cooksons that the raid was coming.

Politicians wanted to avoid a big gun-battle that would infuriate kin and voters.

"Everyone knows that cash buys that kind of consideration," Honey said. "Right, Cecil?"

"He who has enough money can eat sherbet in hell," Cecil said.

•

SOMEWHERE IN OHIO – Saturday, March 3, 1934

Driving back to Chicago from Ohio on another failed stakeout, Lee, Honey and Cecil listened to the latest invention, a radio installed in the dashboard. Some cowboy walloped a guitar and yodeled for little doggies to git along.

"We interrupt this program," the baritone radio announcer said. "Special attention to the Midwestern states. John Dillinger has broken jail in Crown Point, Indiana. He has stolen a sheriff's car and crossed the state line into Illinois."

Cecil whooped and hit the horn. Honey laughed until his eyes turned to slits in his face. He reached under the seat for his bourbon jar and sloshed some down.

"He took the car!" Honey shouted. "ITSMV, interstate transportation of a stolen motor vehicle. Federal law, kid. That means us. Hear that, my little Yalie?"

"He can rob 40 banks and kill cops," Cecil said. "Those aren't federal crimes yet. But as soon as someone takes a car or a dame across state lines without permission, we jump in."

"All hostages said that Dillinger seemed in high spirits," the radio announcer continued. "They said he kept singing '*I'm Heading For the Last Roundup*', the current top hit chart on this station."

"We will settle his hash," Honey said. "Fix his ass good. No more assignments to 'monitor' him. Once we put him away, this country will back the Bureau for the first time ever."

Cecil stepped on the gas and they were racing over the flat plains to Chicago. Honey passed the whiskey. Soon they were all singing *"I'm Heading For the Last Roundup"*

•

MANITOWISH WATERS, WISCONSIN – Friday, April 20, 1934

The countryside was still bedded down from the long Depression winter. Spring came slowly to the woods around Little Star Lake in the North Woods of Wisconsin. Patches of snow lingered into April.

Little Bohemia was isolated on a knuckle of land and surrounded by three lakes, Spider Lake at the back, Little Star at the front, and Manitowish Lake two hundred yards below the inn. U.S. Route 51 wound its way through thick woods and little-known lakes, a quarter mile from the lodge. There were logging roads spiraling back into the fir forests.

The second floor boasted comfortable feather beds for hunters and fishermen. Downstairs, the lodge had a small kitchen, a dining room with a bar, and a living room.

The lodge stayed quiet at this time of year. A few traveling salesmen dribbled through.

FDR had started a work project for young men called the Civilian Conservation Corps, and they had a camp near Little Bohemia. The CCC boys came over to the lodge for the Sunday night special, a chicken dinner for a dollar.

Late that afternoon, four cars swung into the Little Bohemia grounds. Baby Face Nelson sat with his young wife Helen in the lead car, a Ford Tudor sedan. Dillinger, his hair now dyed red and sporting a small fake moustache, followed in a Pontiac Roadster.

Two good-time girls squeezed in the seat beside him. Four more gunmen and their girlfriends trailed them, looking for cops.

The gang needed a place to hole up for a while. Some place without any local cops or federal heat. They had all driven the 370 miles up from Chicago to scout out the lodge, well known to the big shots in Chicago.

The owner, Emil Wanatka, had clawed his way over from Czechoslovakia in the World War. He had turned middleweight professional boxer and then a barkeep and restaurant man during Prohibition in Chicago. All the hoods knew him as a guy who knew how to turn a buck. Gangsters and their women trusted Wanatka to dummy up around the law.

Nelson got out first and checked Little Star Lake.

Lithe and neat, he strutted like a street fighter with a chip on his shoulder. He always seemed in a hurry. Dark hair formed a widow's peak under the round newsboy cap that he always wore.

He got his nickname from the smooth, unmarked face that made him look like a high school kid. Bartenders still asked for proof of age. But under his car coat, a sawed-off shotgun, ten inches long, hung in a shoulder sling. He could whip the shotgun up one-handed and blow off any law-dog's head. Extra shells rolled in his pockets.

He smiled and nodded to the others. The boys would like this place.

It was peaceful, and nobody could bottle them up here.

●

CHICAGO, ILLINOIS – Saturday, April 21, 1934

That day, Lee Childress Senior was in Chicago to visit his son. They had a big steak dinner in the Loop and sat around in Lee's room afterward catching up on old times. Lee sniffed his father's aftershave and the fresh rubber heels of his Florsheim shoes. Lee's Pop nursed a bottle of Hamm's beer while he brought Lee up to date on the family.

His brothers were farming small spreads of their own and doing well. Hard times were keeping people on the farm where they would always have food to live on. Nobody wanted to gamble on a job in the city.

"I'm the only one doing that, right, Pop?"

"Well, might be, might be." Lee's Pop laughed and muttered something about "nerves."

Lee's head snapped up.

"What did you say, Pop?"

"Just that this job's giving your nerves a shellacking. I can tell you have trouble sleeping. The food you eat on the run probably won't agree with your digestion." He took in his son's face over the top of his eyeglasses. "Already started, hasn't it?"

Lee could not look at him.

"In Oklahoma," Lee admitted.

"I was afraid of that. You've always been a nervous little guy. Studying for law school, getting ready for a fight at the gym, you'd burn yourself up worrying about it. I'm too lazy to fret."

"I can't leave the Bureau because of my nerves," Lee said. "That's how everyone would know me. 'The guy who could not cut it'."

"I wouldn't worry about what people say. They always manage to say something. Who cares? Have you thought about what's going to happen if you get into a gunfight, and you're not ready for it? If you can't handle this strain, you could wind up getting yourself and some other agent killed. Would you want that on your conscience?"

"Congress lets us carry guns now, Pop. The voters are supporting us.

Lee's Pop leaned closer.

"This job isn't for you. They're paying you peanuts to do what experienced policemen are afraid to do. You're getting less and less sleep. Need coffee in the morning to get you up and a drink or two at night to bed you down, don't you? I can figure out the rest from your letters."

His eyes flashed.

"This is important to me so I did some dickering. Will Keithly will take you back on. Only this time, you won't be his clerk. You'll be a lawyer working with him. And the money will reflect that."

"You did all this horse-trading and then came here for a visit?"

"I told you it was part business, part pleasure, my being in Chicago."

"I've got to start paying more attention to what you say."

"You can start that back at home," Lee's Pop grinned. "You went to school to be a lawyer. Now you can practice. What do you say?"

Lee hesitated. Then he put both hands in his side pockets and drew them out. His right hand held the Colt 45 sawed-off, pointed at the floor. The other hand cupped the gold badge, a delicate gold sliver, the size of Lee's palm. That same angry bald eagle topped the badge, with the stamped words BUREAU OF INVESTIGATION / U.S. DEPARTMENT OF JUSTICE.

"I've already been in a gunfight," Lee proclaimed. "And I didn't do too badly."

So Lee Childress Senior spent his first night in Chicago watching his son, now lost to him.

CHAPTER 24: Sunday, April 22, 1934

CHICAGO, ILLINOIS

The next day was Sunday and Melvin Purvis was at home in his apartment on Chicago's Gold Coast, smoking a cigar on his balcony. He looked out over Lake Michigan and saw the clouds gathering. A chilling wind rattled down from the north. It was a good time to curl up with a book indoors.

The telephone rang. Purvis stepped back inside to pick up the receiver.

"The man you want most is up here," said the voice on the other end.

"Who's this?"

"Voss, Mr. Purvis. Henry Voss. My sister owns a lodge up on Lake Manitowish."

"Do you mean Dillinger?" Purvis was shaken. His voice showed it. "Where are you calling from? Where is he?"

"I'm in a settlement near Mercer, Wisconsin."

Purvis had never been in Wisconsin in his life and had never heard of Mercer.

"Who is with Dillinger?" Purvis asked.

"Five hoods. And some whores. Gunned up to their eyebrows."

"Where is the nearest airport?"

"None in Manitowish, Mr. Purvis. Nearest one is in Rhinelander."

"Can you do us a favor? Rent five cars for us from an agency."

"Agency shut down about three years ago."

"Then please get five cars from your friends, Mr. Voss. The U.S. government will reimburse you"

"Yes, sir."

"Drive to the airport and wait for us. Wear a white handkerchief on your collar so I'll know you."

Purvis hung up. Then he dialed the Director's line in Washington, D.C.

He snapped his fingers, waiting for J. Edgar Hoover to pick up the telephone. His face in the mirror looked young and untried. There were so many things that could go wrong.

Hoover came on the line and Purvis filled him in.

"This sounds promising," the Director said. "Now, Saint Paul, Minnesota, is closer to Rhinelander than Chicago is. Contact Inspector Clegg in the Saint Paul field office. He's an Assistant Director and will be in charge of this entire operation."

Purvis grimaced. His fingers tightened and bent his smoking cigar. Someone else would take the responsibility.

"I know about the local constables in a place like Rhinelander," Hoover went on. "They won't help you in an operation like this. They might be protecting Dillinger's gang. Remember what happened in Kansas City. If you tip the police off, the gang might slaughter you on the road. Dillinger has been making a fool of the Bureau. So this raid will be a Bureau operation, from start to finish. I hope you understand that."

"Yessir, Mister Director," Purvis said.

Purvis waited to hear Hoover hang up the phone. He realized that he was standing erect, like a first-year plebe at his military academy.

"Something wrong, boss?" President, the houseboy asked. His black face twisted in a fret.

Purvis dialed Hollis, still standing straight.

"I'm running this raid, not that fat Mississippi show-boat Clegg," Purvis said.

"Yessir," President said. "You and me are South Carolina gentlemen, from the Low Country. I ain't studying no Mississippi gentleman. I got my dignity, and you got yours. You in charge, sir."

"Whoever pulls this one off is set for life in the Bureau," Purvis said.

"Yessir."

"Now you're saying to me just what I said to Mister Hoover."

"Yessir."

●

Around six that evening, agents from all over Chicago streamed into the Municipal Airport, They lugged the new issue equipment of Tommy guns, shotguns, tear gas launchers and heavy steel bullet-proof vests with leather straps.

Honey had been training some of the agents at the police range. Others were still waiting for their first class.

At seven that evening, Purvis met them outside the airplane hangar next to the Administration building. The sun was setting as he told them it was still winter in the North Woods and they were going into unknown territory. The wind whipped at them as they huddled next to each other.

Purvis scanned the agents. His gray eyes looked boyish and bright. His years as a cadet leader, burnished with dead Rebel kinfolk at Gettysburg, came back to him.

"Gentlemen, we have Johnnie Dillinger located at a lodge in upper Wisconsin. I'll be picking a raiding party from the agents assembled here."

An airplane's roar drowned him out.

"Look down that runway," Homer Bisbee said. "What do you see?"

"Nothing, simple. It's too dark to see."

"It's too dark to see in the Wisconsin woods, too," Homer Bisbee said. "We are heading into the unknown."

"We got no plan and no juice," Homer Bisbee said. "Families might lose their daddies tonight."

The men stirred in their long winter coats, with suits and ties and white dress shirts underneath. They felt the cold.

"You're right," someone said. In the dark, Lee could not see his face. "All we got are guts and the Bureau."

"Hush up. Mr. Purvis is stepping near."

They fixed dull looks on their faces.

"We can't wait any longer for the others to arrive," Purvis said. "Dillinger plans to leave tonight. We'll be doing this without any police help."

Purvis checked a list on the back of an envelope and began calling out names.

"Winstead and Ross, my two soldiers and Texas Rangers, will you get on the plane, please?" Purvis asked.

"Me, too, Boss," McQueeny said.

"We need everyone there," Cecil said.

"Bow-wow, Yale!" Honey hissed.

Purvis looked down the runway.

"Mr. Laughlin," Purvis said. "I'm running this operation and I'm making this somewhat voluntary. Everyone knows that we are not trained for this. Some should stay here and coordinate."

"Not me," Baum said, a husky football athlete with that flat accent from Spokane. His sandy hair, parted in the middle, waved in the wind. "I want to do real police work, Mr. Purvis."

"I'm making the list, sir," Purvis said.

He passed over a few names. Those agents looked relieved.

Cecil locked eyes with Purvis. Cecil's cigar glow lit up his face. Purvis motioned him over to the plane's staircase and also fingered Ed Hollis.

Hollis picked up two pump shotguns.

"Mr. Ross says that he's seen you shoot good scores on the shotgun, Mr. Hollis," Purvis said. "Let's see. Who else? You come too, Mr. Childress."

Purvis motioned to Lee.

Lee's gut sucked in. He nodded, squinting against the pain. One shoe followed another and he walked stiff-legged behind the other men towards two chartered Northrop Delta planes on the runway.

The men left behind watched the agents board the planes. They were relieved at not going. They tried to hide it.

●

Filled with agents, the two airplanes rumbled down the runway and took off. The pilots were winging it, too. They were leather-jacketed barnstormers who flew by the seat of their pants, using only road maps to guide them to Rhinelander.

A bitter wind chilled the men sitting next to their black leather gun cases. Some blew on their fingers to keep them warm and wondered how many of them would be coming back.

●

For two hours, they flew into cold. The planes shook their bones and landed at the tiny Rhinelander air field. Night had fallen. The temperature was dropping rapidly. A wall thermometer read 22 degrees.

The plane's prop was still whirling as the agents clambered out, holding their gun cases.

A thin man with pure white hair hastened across the tarmac. He wore a white handkerchief around his neck .

"Mr. Purvis! Mr. Purvis!" the handkerchief man shouted.

Purvis stopped and put out his hand.

"I'm Henry Voss," the man panted as he shook Purvis's hand.

As they walked toward the wood-frame hangar, Purvis signaled Voss to silence. Purvis fretted about leaks.

"Stay close to me, kid," Honey said to Lee as they climbed out of the plane. "This might turn into a mess."

He lit up his stogie and offered Lee a fresh one.

Lee felt sick from the plane ride. He shook his head. He was trying to slow down his heart, racing like a car engine with nowhere to go.

"That's Inspector Clegg," said Honey. He pointed across the runway. The Chicago agents knew the Inspector by sight – a chunky, slow-moving man dressed for the cold in a tattersall hunting coat with leather patches. A team of agents from Clegg's office trailed him.

Since nothing ever happened in Rhinelander, the locals stood around, watching, One fellow in a gray sweatshirt stamped with the CCC pine tree logo asked Cecil who they were.

"Wedding party band," Cecil said, as he lifted out a gun case that looked like a leather trombone case. "Just a band from Chicago, 'bo. Know anyplace in town where they got good champagne?"

·

Voss had hired the only five cars he could find. They were a white Packard sedan and Ford, Chevy and Plymouth sedans. They looked like they were driven hard on the country roads and neglected. He also loaned Purvis a 1929 Cunningham hearse.

Voss watched the silent agents load their gear into the hearse.

Purvis, Voss and Clegg got into the Packard along with the driver Baum. Homer Bisbee drove the hearse. Honey climbed into the Ford sedan with McQueeny, Winstead and Lee. Lee tried to ignore the hearse and what it meant.

"This whole operation is very sloppy," Lee said.

"Well, it's going to get even sloppier," Honey sneered. "Dillinger won't say 'uncle'. There's bound to be some fireworks."

"Bound to be."

Lee looked over his shoulder to see that it was McQueeny talking. McQueeny's white hair sticking up in back. His drinker's face looked lined and tired.

"Johnnie will fight because we've got no reputation as shooters," McQueeny said. "He thinks he'll get away. I'm not trained for this. None of us are. But, by golly, we're going to stop him this time."

Lee studied McQueeny, the loud-talking oldster and political stooge. Lee used to see him as useless. But McQueeny did not look useless now.

"You really think we could swing this?" Lee asked. "Without the local sheriff?"

"Nobody called them," McQueeny said. "Nobody trusts them. The guy with the handkerchief called us because he trusts us. Finally, all this work on our image, all this apple-polishing in business suits, this public relations jazz, is starting to pay off."

Purvis gave the signal. The five cars pushed off into the black night. Before they had gone three miles, the cold froze everyone.

Honey drove, using all his skill to keep on the rutted road. He sang through his chattering teeth, "*I'm Heading For the Last Roundup.*"

"My favorite song," Honey said. "Johnnie's favorite, too." There were no houses anywhere in sight and no other cars on the road. Mile after mile, they passed icy pines and frozen evergreens.

The Ford lurched and the engine quit. Honey cursed.

He stepped out and raised the hood. He fiddled with the carburetor and the spark plug wires.

But when he tried to start it, the engine lay dead.

The next car pulled up behind it, a sea-green 1929 Plymouth sedan with Suran at the wheel. Suran helped Honey and the others transfer the vests and gun-cases into it.

The agents inside rolled the windows down. Honey and McQueeny stepped in snow and up onto the running board. Lee hesitated. Honey looked at Lee. Lee joined them on the running board. They held onto the window frames on as the car pulled out, fingers frozen in the bitter night air.

Twenty minutes later, the Chevy sedan bucked and stopped. The engine ground.

"That stump-broke mama mule car dealer!" Honey cussed. "What kinda rolling trash he give us? Go back, walk up on one side of his ass and down the other."

More agents got on the running boards and gripped whatever they could.

McQueeny was sneezing nonstop. The agents bounced around on the running boards. It took everything they had just to hang on.

Lee's temples pounded. He coughed deeply and doubled over from it. It felt like something sharp in his throat and chest. He spat up something that looked greenish in the darkness.

They bounced and skidded. Bodies slammed into each other. Icy winds knifed through the proper business suits. Wind nibbled trouser cuffs.

Lee slipped on the running board and lost his balance. He managed to cling to the car as the wind cut him again. He closed his eyes against it.

"Can't do this," he chanted so nobody else could hear. "Oh, this is awful, awful."

The car kept jolting him.

Purvis stopped the lead car and cut his lights. The remaining two cars did the same. Lee took out his spectacles and made out the lights of two buildings through pine trees.

"Keep them coke bottles on, kid," said Honey. "That's the Little Bohemia Lodge most likely."

He pointed to the shimmering waters of Spider Lake.

"The place is surrounded by water. Johnnie can't get away. We got him boxed sweet."

Purvis held a whispered conference on the road's shoulder. He wanted a covering party to fire as the raiding party moved in. He put Lee in the covering party. Hollis handed Lee a shotgun. Lee's hands still shook from gripping the car frame and he wondered how the others were feeling.

"But we wait now, gentlemen," Purvis said. His Carolina drawl thickened from pressure. "More agents are racing here. We do not move unless the subjects try to leave."

Lee and the agents spread out along the lodge property. He checked his shotgun, a pump action Winchester that held five shells, jamming the extra shells into the right hand pocket of his suit jacket.

He got himself set and ready for anything. Left hand to slide forward and the right hand to feed shells from the pocket into the breech. It was just like hunting ducks with the old man back home.

Cecil passed by him, holding a Tommy pointed at the ground. Snow patches showed.

"Nothing to be nervous about, kid," Cecil said, his mood happy. "You know how much I like Shakespeare. Well, in just a few hours, it'll be April 23, Shakespeare's birthday. Why don't we both nail Johnnie as a birthday present for the Bard?"

Lee nodded and sank into a crouch on the frozen ground.

"Hanging onto that car, waiting for shots took everything out of me."

"You'll do okay," Cecil said and left.

Nerves still shook Lee's hands. They twitched to throw down his shotgun so he could run into the woods to hide.

Lee could see the two-story frame houses clearly through the trees. His heart and breath were slamming against his chest. The fear was worse than anything in Oklahoma.

He knew he was going to die. He thought about the last time he had walked on the Shad Road on a winter evening.

Chapter 25: Sunday, April 22, 1934
A Short Time Later

LITTLE BOHEMIA, WISCONSIN

Purvis and Clegg held Tommy guns. Lee stood thirty yards from the flickering lights of the lodge. Behind them, agents Baum and Newman clustered with gun barrels bristling over winter topcoats. Newman fixed his glasses, his thin scholar's face pale in the cold. A blond cowlick rose from his head.

The front door opened. A group of men crowded out of the lodge. They moved to a Buick coupe.

Lee gagged. The shotgun dangled in his hands.

"That's Dillinger," McQueeny hissed.

"He's getting away!" whispered Lee.

"Our guys are still getting in place," Purvis said. "We don't have enough."

"They'll be gone in a minute!" said Lee.

"Come on, Nervous Purvis!" Honey urged.

"We wait," Purvis said.

"Make a decision!" snapped Honey.

"Move in!" Purvis said.

He waved his Tommy gun and pointed at the Buick.

The agents started running, sliding through the mud and snow. Guns and bullet-proof vests weighed them down. Near the lodge, a dog barked. Another dog howled. They looked like collies. Lee could see them plunging on their leashes.

The men in the lodge parking lot got inside the Buick. When the engine caught, the dogs howled more.

"They're getting away!" McQueeny said.

The Buick sped up.

"Aim for the tires!" Purvis shouted. "You there! Federal officers! Halt!"

Purvis triggered his Thompson.

Gunfire spurted from the woods. Bullet tracer streams hit the car. Cecil was ten feet from the lodge when he hit the dirt, holding his fire. The car windows shattered and the men inside it slumped down, shouting. One of them ran back inside the lodge.

"Hands up!"

Someone fired back from the lodge. Then two more gunners opened up with Tommies. The collies howled. Bullets chopped up the forest floor near the agents. Dillinger had been ready.

Cecil ran closer from hiding somewhere and blasted the second floor windows. Winstead ran up, leaped behind a tree and fired his shotgun. Lee racked one shell into the breech, fired, racked another one, and fired. The lodge lights went out. Hollis humped across the driveway and got behind an elm tree.

Another Tommy chattered from the ground floor window. Lee shouldered the shotgun and fired buckshot right into the window. He saw Purvis and Clegg, belly-down, waving their Tommy guns over the lodge front. The return fire had stopped. One body was stretched flat by the car.

"They're still in the lodge!" Purvis shouted. "We've got them. Nobody gets out!"

McQueeny nodded and ran past, carrying his shotgun against his hip. Honey was coming in from the flank, his Winchester .30-30 lever-action blazing.

Holding his Tommy gun, Purvis ripped open the Buick door. A man's head, pince-nez eyeglasses broken and blood-spattered on it, sagged from the shoulders.

"Tumbling Tumbleweeds" played from the car radio.

"That's not Dillinger," Purvis said. "Civilian Conservation Corps uniform. I know Johnnie's face."

"Somebody shot too high?" Lee said.

"I did," Baum said. "My Thompson climbed."

Baum stared between the victim and his machine gun.

"He was innocent," Baum said. "I killed him."

"Nobody knows that, Baum," Purvis said. "Buck up. We got work to do. They're trapped inside.

"I'll never shoot one of these again," Baum said. He dropped the Tommy gun onto the dirt. "I'm done."

"I'll tell you when you're done," Purvis said. "Nobody sits this one out. Pick up that gun."

"Nobody trained Baum on the Tommy," Honey said. "We never got the time to do it. It's not his fault."

Tears smeared Baum's cheeks in the yellowish light from the lodge.

A man inside the car groaned. He held his gut. Blood showed pink intestines against his green work shirt. Lee heard whimpering. He saw a third man hiding under the dashboard. Blood ran down his arm.

"That was '*Tumbling Tumbleweeds*' by Sons of the Pioneers," the faraway voice of the disk jockey said on the car radio. "And now for something a little different by Jimmy Durante."

"Inka-Dinka-Doo" began to play.

"Gotta take care of them!" Lee said.

The groaning man's breathing rasped. Honey leaned over and took the man's hand.

"Easy, partner," Honey said. "You be okay."

The man's head slumped.

"He's just out," Honey said. "He'll make it."

Headlights swept the road, then suddenly a spotlight illuminated the agents.

They scattered back into the shadows as an older Plymouth sedan with a small white star stenciled on its side pulled up.

"Cut those lights!" Cecil hollered.

"Who you, boy?" a man shouted from the car. "I'm Constable Christensen, Spider Lake. Nobody runs my territory but me."

The lights went out.

A patch of wavy inky hair showed over the constable's rubbery face as he clambered out of the car. Like many of the locals, he looked part Chippewa. A tin star flashed next to the stag-handled Colt Peacemaker cowboy revolver on his hip.

"Lord, we got us a museum exhibit here," McQueeny said "They still leave relics like him run around the countryside?".

"Bureau of Investigation," Honey said. His creds case flapped open. "We got Johnnie Dillinger inside the house there.

"You got Dillinger?" the constable said. "I can't believe it."

"Me, neither," Homer Bisbee said.

"They just elected me six weeks ago," the constable said. "And here I am with Johnnie 'Bigger-Than-Life' Dillinger."

"Isn't life just wonderful?" Cecil said.

Purvis snapped his fingers at Baum and Newman. Newman's eyeglasses showed mud from diving to the ground.

"Where's the nearest phone?" Purvis asked Christensen.

"Koerner's place," Christensen said. "Up the road a piece."

"Newman, take your car," Purvis said.

"Yessir."

"Use their phone to get help here fast," Purvis said. "We need to set up local roadblocks."

"Call who?"

"The Rhinelander Airport," Purvis said. His voice climbed. "Tell the controller when more agents land to send them out here. Immediately. We need reinforcements. Then call the director. Notify him that the criminals are still trapped in the lodge. They're not getting away this time."

"I'll go, all right," Baum said. "I'm washed up here."

"Hush up that noise, mister," Purvis said. "I'm in command here. Any mistakes made are mine. Nobody else. That's the discipline we obey."

"Come on, Baum," said Newman as he headed towards his car.

"They'll never find Koerner's in the dark," the constable said. "Better take my car."

Newman and Baum looked to Purvis.

"And even if they do find him," Christensen added, "Koerner will think that he's just a-nightmaring. He needs to see me."

Purvis nodded.

They trio jumped into the Plymouth, and Christensen gunned it.

●

They drove down a country lane flanked by white post and rail fences.

"I think that we should stay put," Newman said. "If our Mr. Purvis wants to telephone the Director, let him make the call."

Baum just looked out the window. Newman saw the tear streaks on his cheeks.

"You G-men, this is your first raid?" the constable asked.

"This is everyone's first raid," Newman said. "And if we get the Director down here, it will be his first raid. We're all doing this by copying Tom Mix cowboy movies."

Newman saw Baum shaking his head.

Christensen pulled up beside the gate marked "Koerner's."

"And don't ask me about my experience in shoot-outs," Newman said. "I'm a Mormon Lay Preacher from Salt Lake City."

Koerner's home was a wood-frame bungalow with a gabled upstairs. Pines and a tall birch tree grouped nearby. A gray Packard sat in the driveway.

"That's Koerner's car all right," Christensen said. "Probably heard the noise."

"Baum, jot down the plate, will you?" Newman said.

Christensen drove. Baum put down his Tommy to write.

Thirty feet past the Packard, there was another parked car, a maroon Ford crowded with bodies.

Christensen pulled up flush alongside it.

"Hello, there," Newman said. "I'm looking for Mister Koerner."

The Ford's doors flew open. People burst out. They screamed. Someone waved a pistol. He looked like a kid.

"Baum!" Newman shouted. "Gun him!"

"What?" Baum said.

Shots roared. Glass blew out. The horn blared. Baum's throat exploded blood and tissue. Something wet covered Newman's glasses. He pushed himself from the car. Newman felt something smack his head.

"I'm Baby Face Nelson!" the kid screamed. "You bastards are wearing vests! I give it to you high and low!"

Baum fell against the seat. The kid fired more. Baum staggered out of the car.

He tried to bring his Tommy up. Christensen lay still across the ground.

"You're trying to kill me!" the kid screamed.

The kid clambered into the Ford.

Baum collapsed.

Newman rolled over in the snowy mud. His .38 dangled in his hand. He fired prone. The slug smacked the vent next to the kid's head. The kid fired back. He jammed a clip into the gun and fired. He missed.

Newman shot a volley.

He hit the hood and the side window. Slugs blew apart the mirror.

Baum groaned alongside.

Newman inhaled. He remembered Honey's training on the pistol range. He braced himself for one last shot. He fired. His gun bucked. The slug missed. The Ford roared away.

Newman's eyes rolled back.

•

By four in the morning the locals were all over Little Bohemia. They all wanted to see Dillinger or shoot him. Either one was okay with them. The crowd turned into vigilantes, taking pot shots at the lodge. When Purvis ordered them to leave, they laughed at him. They figured the feds had no power here.

The local sheriff was on hand, watching the show. His face looked like a chunk of leather left out in the snow and then dried out by the sun. Thick moustaches covered his upper lip.

Hollis lobbed three tear gas candles into the lodge and the fumes curled out of the smashed windows. Nobody had fired back from the lodge since the first volley.

"The gang is probably in the basement," Purvis said.

His voice sounded hoarse from shouting surrender deals.

Little Star Lake began to turn gray just before the sun rose. Lee and Honey were drenched from lying on the snowy ground and their teeth chattered. Exhausted, they smoked stogies to keep awake.

The sheriff had taken two wounded strangers from the car to his jeep. A doctor fixed their wounds.

"Let me get them ridden over to the county hospital," the sheriff said.

"They are in federal custody," Purvis said. "We don't even know who they are, yet. The doctor said that they can wait a bit longer."

The third man lay dead in front of the lodge. Snow mixed with blood on his uniform shirt.

Someone came running over from Route 51, shouting. He was a bulldog-type, sweating like he had been running for miles. Cecil hustled him to Purvis.

"All your men are dead," the man wheezed.

"What's your name?"

"Listen, you simple son-of-a-bitch, did you come for me or for Dillinger? I'm Wanatka, and I own the place. Let me tell you something, big shot. Dillinger left last night. You're shooting into an empty house!"

"We've had the house surrounded."

"You had nothing surrounded! You can't see the shoreline from here. If you'd asked anyone here, they would have told you. Dillinger just came out the back windows, ran down to the shoreline and kept running until he got into the woods. You want to know who I am? That's my lodge you're shooting up. Sheriff, you know me. Tell this guy I'm telling the truth. Dillinger's boys shot back and ran."

Purvis's face tightened.

"Then who were the guys who tried to get away in their car?" Purvis asked.

"Customers from the CCC camp. You see the uniforms, right?"

"Were they helping Dillinger?"

"You're so messed up that Dillinger didn't need any help. These boys aren't crooks. They just didn't know who you were. Drinking some beers with dinner. What would you do if some jokers without uniforms on jumped out from the trees at night, waving guns?"

"We identified ourselves."

"By words? No badges. I been around and know the boys in Chicago."

"I'll bet you do," Purvis said.

"They won't stop for words unless there's a badge with them. Neither would you. If you had the sheriff in uniform with you, they would have stopped. So you shot them."

The agents said nothing.

"The sheriff wouldn't know them because they stay at their CCC camp," Wanatka said. "I was at Koerner's when the shooting started and some little crook ran from here to Koerner's and pushed us all in a car. When your men showed up there, this little guy shot them down like clay pigeons. Koerner saw it all. He told me."

As though on cue, the basement door opened. The agents shouted and took aim. A bulldog pup trotted out, followed by three women, hands high over their heads, white handkerchiefs waving. The tear gas had taken a long time to work and they were all crying from the fumes.

The sheriff leaned toward Purvis. "You mean to tell me that's all you got? No Dillinger?"

"We'll check."

"The radio said your boss Hoover in Washington called the newspapers and told them you had Dillinger surrounded. He couldn't get away. Ha! You got innocent people and your own men killed. You got no authority for this mess. You'll be lucky if you don't end in jail yourself."

●

Purvis motioned the agents into the lodge. They checked under the beds and inside the closets but the lodge was empty. The men came back outside coughing from the tear gas and put their heads under a water pump.

The sheriff impounded their rented cars for what he called "investigation," and the agents had to walk six miles to the nearest village, carrying their equipment.

CHAPTER 26: Thursday, May 3, 1934

CHICAGO, ILLINOIS

The spring weather came in fine and warm after Little Bohemia, and one afternoon Lee knocked off early and went home with Honey for dinner. Lee chewed coffee beans. They covered up his wine breath from last night's drinking.

Lee sat with Honey's wife Jan on the front porch, looking out on Stony Island Avenue while Honey cooked steaks inside the kitchen. Doing nothing made Lee toss his head back to doze.

"So Baum is dead?" Jan asked.

"Yes. He died at Koerner's house."

"How about the others?"

"Newman survived, even though he was shot in the head. The village constable pulled through, but he's crippled for life. Nelson shot him six times. Baum took a long time to die, lying there wounded in the snow."

Jan shook her head.

"Nelson must be crazy," she said.

Lee remembered what Honey had said about Nelson.

"He likes to shoot, all right. Nelson doesn't act normal, even for a hood. He's kill-crazy. He'll attack a lawman whenever he can. He'll take out some more of us or die trying, you can bet on that. And nobody who reads the papers hears about that. The papers have him as a poor, misunderstood youth who just panicked when the fellas started throwing their weight around. It's enough to make you toss your cookies."

"You sound like you want to quit, Lee. When are you resigning?"

"When we get Nelson. When we get Dillinger. When we get Pretty Boy Floyd."

"Honey's tense and short of breath all the time," Jan said. "Two agents had nervous breakdowns already. You boys are pounding down way too much joy juice for men your age. He's showing all the signs for a heart attack."

"Nobody mentioned breakdowns."

"The Bureau covers up to create the image. They want Mr. and Mrs. America to think that you boys go to bed laughing and wake up singing. You are the first showboat, clean-cut police in America. Mr. Hoover will never admit that he is putting you all through hell to sell the image."

"Do you know what Will Rogers says?" she asked. "It's in the paper here.

'Well, they had Dillinger surrounded and they was all ready to shoot him when he came out. But another bunch of innocent folks came out first, so they shot them instead. Dillinger is going to accidentally get with some innocent bystanders some time, then he will get shot.'"

"We got some gains out of that Bohemia mess," Lee said. "Thanks to the Crime Bill, it's now a federal offense to assault or kill one of us. We're allowed to go after crooks anywhere and make legal arrests. We can carry Tommies, Winchester shotguns, the new Monitor automatic rifle, a Remington .30 rifle."

"Ray Caffrey and Carter Baum had a lot to do with getting that bill passed, from what I hear," she said. "There'll be some other agents dead before it's over. I want H.T. to leave Chicago and get back to Texas. The kids and I don't like it here. H.T. can get a marshal's job down there, and I can always find work."

Honey came out with two frosty steins of beer and set them down on the porch table.

"I'll be right back," he said. "I have to make an important telephone call."

He went back to the kitchen and dialed the phone. They heard his voice change to an aging whine.

"Chicago? Yes, I want to speak to Special Agent Homer Bisbee. Oh, he isn't . . . You tell Agent Homer Bisbee when you find him that Inspector Nathan from Washington, D.C. is trying to locate him. He's supposed to be at his desk until six o'clock each day. What do I want to talk to him about? Same as before. It's about those car accidents. You tell him next time he's in an accident on Bureau time, he damn well better report it."

●

Dillinger was staying away from banks and the family farm at Mooresville. The feds had the farm covered for real now. His gang had scattered after Little Bohemia.

He settled into a rooming house at 3967 Pine Grove Avenue, in the Mid North section of Chicago. Every morning, he bought the Chicago Tribune and had a shave at the Lincoln Avenue barber shop.

Dillinger was using the name Jimmy Lawrence.

To his barber and his neighbors on Pine Grove Avenue, Jimmy Lawrence was a clerk at the Chicago Board of Trade. Plastic surgery had changed Dillinger's looks. A scar on his upper lip was gone, his cleft chin was smooth, his cheeks were leaner and his nose was shorter. He had a thick moustache and kept his hair clipped short. He wore gold-rimmed eyeglasses everywhere he went.

This formed his summer period, the last one that he would ever enjoy. The bank-robberies and Tommy gun battles felt like they belonged to another man. He knew that his only chance was to lay low and blend in with the sleepy neighborhood sweating through the summer.

His senses slowed. He could find appreciation in just watching a mutt amble down a sticky sidewalk, looking for shade. Dillinger felt like that mutt. Both of them needed to be left alone.

The old Dillinger face was in all the tabloids, the hair combed straight back, pug nose, and crooked grin.

Dillinger talked with Louie Piquette, his mouthpiece lawyer, a few times in the crowd at Wrigley Field. Piquette looked well-fed, with light gray hair combed into a crest. The brown pinstripe suit draped over his bowling-ball belly. A butter-colored necktie flared against the broadcloth white shirt. He kept in touch with Dillinger's girlfriends. He sampled a few of them. The girlfriends knew how to do things that Mrs. Piquette never imagined.

Piquette told Dillinger that the cops were busy tailing all the women he had ever known and shaking them down for information. Dillinger grinned and did not care. Nobody knew where to look for him in his sleepy neighborhood.

Baby Face Nelson sent word through his mouthpiece that he wanted to work some more jobs. Dillinger stayed away from him. Nelson was too hot after slaughtering that Fed Baum.

Dillinger started dating a waitress named Polly in the neighborhood. Polly's body showed sleek flanks over long showgirl legs. Ropy dark hair worn loose framed high cheekbones and a wide mouth made for kissing.

He kept dickering with Piquette about escaping out of the country. The mouthpiece found a couple who were taking a trip to Mexico. Johnnie liked the sound of Mexico. He met with the couple, and they did not recognize him from the papers. For ten grand, they would bring him into Mexico as their son.

Piquette covered the passport angle. They made plans to leave on Monday morning, July 23rd. They would have no trouble getting into Mexico.

●

The pressure built to find Dillinger. Cops and FBI men criss-crossed Chicago, looking for him. They tailed Piquette whenever they could keep him in sight.

Congressmen got so angry that they forgot their clichés. They demanded to know what the Bureau was doing to find him. Purvis's men worked around the clock, sitting in parked cars on long stakeouts and following street characters who were friendly to the gang.

CHAPTER 27: Sunday, July 22, 1934

CHICAGO, ILLINOIS

A heat wave flattened the city that Sunday afternoon. Lee came into the field office to write up surveillance reports on Dillinger's friends, Mary Longaker, now living in Chicago, and Jimmy Probasco. Lee found Honey and Cecil hustling two hand-cuffed prisoners into the bullpen. One was Piquette, Dillinger's lawyer. Lee knew him from the newspapers.

The second prisoner was Billie, her dark heavy hair tied back against the heat and wearing a wheat-colored light summer dress. Lee's face pinked up. He took off his glasses and saw steam on the lenses.

As usual, Honey was excited about making a collar. His drawl slurred his words.

He dumped the prisoners' possessions onto the front desk.

"Both of you are under arrest for harboring a fugitive," he said.

Billie saw Lee looking at her. She winked at him.

"Do you want to make any calls, Evelyn?" Honey asked her.

"Don't call me Evelyn. My friends call me Billie."

"You won't catch Johnnie in Chicago," she went on. "He made a deal with a reporter for the Kansas City Star. For $42,000, Johnnie has done interviews with their ace reporter about his life."

"$42,000? Is someone crazy? Or just real rich?"

"Johnnie got the cash already," Billie said. "He's long gone."

"Why rob banks anymore?" Honey asked.

"I think that's a lot of petrified apple butter," Cecil said. "Cow-flop."

"You mean that Dillinger just floated that story so we would stop looking for him?" Lee asked.

Cecil's mouth tightened as he looked at Lee. Lee saw that another mood was seizing Cecil.

The harsh look made Lee step back.

Billie grinned and tossed her black hair.

If Billie told them about Lee, Lee would be bounced out of the Bureau. The Bureau was run by old maids, with Hoover the biggest old maid of all. Lee's shirt wetted with sweat as Piquette began fussing with Cecil and Honey.

"I'm John Dillinger's lawyer, Louis Piquette, Esquire. That's a matter of court record. The charge of harboring just doesn't apply."

His dark calculating eyes watched as Cecil and Lee brought him into the bullpen and locked the door behind them. Honey stayed outside with Billie.

"We'll get to the law in a minute, counselor," Cecil said. "I'm an attorney myself, and I guarantee you that everything will be done according to proper legal procedure."

"It had better be."

Cecil pivoted on his left foot and snapped a hook into the air. His right hand followed up. His hands never touched Piquette. But the fists came close. Cecil swung another combination.

"That does not scare me," Piquette said. "I used to box professionally."

"It is not my intention to scare you," Cecil said. "Just to let you know what could happen here. Without witnesses. Your client killed a cop, and Nelson killed one of my partners. You are going to the slammer. Meanwhile, I'm going to beat you till you can't walk. I want Johnnie."

Piquette tried to get up. "You . . ."

"Choose your vocabulary with care, counselor. Or else I'll drown you in a butt of Malmsey wine, then go home and sleep like a baby. You can't threaten me. I don't like this lousy Bureau, and for two pins I'd go back to Yale and teach law. Where's Johnnie?"

Piquette looked at Lee. "You can't do this."

"You're right," Lee said. "I can't. But he can."

"Where's Dillinger?" Cecil asked.

"That's privileged."

"I don't want to hear that word from you, scum. You've got no privilege here. All you've got is me in a small room."

Lee coughed but it came up as a sob, His gut heaved with worry about Billie.

●

He left the bullpen and went down the hall to the washroom.

Two strangers with briefcases came down the hall. Their eyes walked over Lee.

"Excuse me," the taller one with slicked back hair and gold pince-nez glasses said. "What is your name, Agent?"

"Childress."

The other one, square and dark in his cream colored suit, scrutinized Lee.

"Excuse me," the square one said. "You did not ask us who we are."

Lee sputtered.

"We're from the Attorney General Cummings' office," the taller one. "We are investigating what went wrong at Little Bohemia."

"And other mistakes," the square one said. "If you were at Little Bohemia, we'll be interviewing you today."

Lee hack-coughed. His body jackknifed.

Both strangers stared at him.

"I have to go," Lee said.

He whipped around and strode away.

His shoes clacked on the floor.

"We'll see you later," one of them said.

Lee escaped into the bathroom and spread his palms across the sink. Inside the suit, his belly heaved again.

He ran cold water over his face and hands, feeling sick. Billie would talk. She would get Purvis's ear and tell him about the nights in Lee's bed.

It might be better for him to resign before Billie talked. That way, he would go out clean. Nobody would ever know.

He pulled open a window and looked out. The Loop swirled underneath him with traffic on a hot Sunday afternoon. He put his glasses on and tried to settle his breathing. The minutes ached by.

"Relax."

Lee spun around.

Honey was standing next to the washbasin, sleeves rolled up over his arms, looking like the village blacksmith.

"She just told me the whole bit, Lee. I sent the steno away. Nobody heard Billie talk. And she won't talk to anyone else."

"How d'you know?" Lee asked.

"Oh, I know. Don't worry. This is my world and my people. I drink too much, borrow money, dally with girls who aren't my wife, gamble with the rent money. I'm just like them but I've got a federal badge. She won't talk. You got that?"

"I didn't know she was Johnnie's girl, Honey," Lee said. "We got her name down as Evelyn Frechette. I only knew her as Billie. If I'd known –"

"You might have planked her anyway. People do what they want to do. Remember that."

"She'll talk."

"Hey, listen to me," Honey said. "She won't talk. Give you my word. She knows what I'd do to her. You and me are not going to talk about this ever again. And you're not going to tell anyone, ever. Lee, this is my fault. I shouldn't have left you by yourself in Borden and Pine's. She said she tagged us as G-men right from the start."

"Did she think that I would protect her?"

"That might have been part of it. I asked her, and she said yes. But you can't ever trust what these street people say, not all of it. I figure you were someone new and different who treated her nice."

"You think that's why she kept seeing me?"

"You may never believe this but I think she saw you because she likes you. It's as simple as that."

Hollis escorted Piquette and Billie to the U.S. marshal's office.

●

The field office rhythm slowed. Everyone tried to beat the heat.

The radio said the mercury had broken the 100-degree mark. No breeze came off the lake front. Seventeen Chicagoans had died from heat prostration the day before.

Honey started to brew a pot of coffee. He was the only die-hard Java drinker who could take a cup in this heat. Footsteps clacked down the hall.

"There goes Cowley," Honey said. "The new Inspector."

"Who is he?" Suran said. "I've been stuck inside a Cicero tool-shed forever, waiting for Dillinger to show up in the park."

"Cowley kind of favors a panda," Honey said. "Roly-poly, with big eyes. He is just a paper-pusher from headquarters. Word says that he cannot qualify on the handgun range. Mister Hoover sent him here to clean up things after our Little Bohemia mess. Remember, some newspapers were calling on Purvis to resign. Cowley's got good nerves, taking on this kind of job. Brave fella. He knows that he ain't ready for it."

NEITHER AM I, Lee thought to himself.

"Purvis offered to quit," McQueeny said. "But that would make the public throw us away. Like Newman, Cowley's a Mormon from Utah. Missionary in Hawaii and speaks their lingo."

"Missionary?"

"Yep. It's useful. If Dillinger shoots you, Cowley can pray over you."

Cowley's jowly face and pale skin appeared in the doorway.

"Get everyone in the bullpen," Cowley said. "Now."

Purvis came through the door quickly and made some phone calls to bring the other agents in. Cowley scanned his notes. Everything he did, he did slowly. Hoover wanted it that way. No more panicky moves by Nervous Purvis.

Winstead and Brown arrived together, then Homer Bisbee, licking an ice cream cone. Hollis came in from the street in his shirt sleeves, wearing sunglasses and a straw hat. His Bureau issued Colt bulged in his pants hip pocket.

"Cecil," Lee whispered. "Where did you learn to threaten like that?"

"Yale."

"You sounded pretty scary."

"Gentlemen, I would like some order," Cowley said in his Western twang. He sketched a street diagram on the blackboard. "Mr. Purvis, will you please bring in our visitors?"

Purvis whipped his head up. Cowley nodded.

"Cowley's showing who is the boss now," someone whispered.

Purvis brought in three strangers. Their clothes were so bad they had to be policemen. Their holsters and handcuff cases creaked whenever they moved.

"Gentlemen," Cowley said. "We've received word that Dillinger will be at the Marbro Theater tonight. He'll be with our informant, Anna Sage, and his girlfriend, a part-time hooker named Polly. We obtained this information with the help of our friends here from the East Chicago Police Department."

Cowley passed out maps of the theater.

"This is the theater and alley," Purvis said. "Each agent has his assigned place, in the alley, covering the rear exits or across the street."

"Anna Sage will be easy to spot," Cowley said. "She'll be wearing a red dress. Remember that, the woman in red."

Purvis stepped closer to the agents. Lee could imagine him as a young Confederate cavalryman in gray, addressing his dragoons before the battle. Purvis' light eyes glittered like he was looking into the future.

"Gentlemen, you all know the character of John Dillinger," Purvis said. "If we locate him and he makes his escape, it will be a disgrace to our Bureau. It may be that Dillinger will be at the picture show with his women companions unarmed.

"But he may appear there armed and with other members of his gang. There will be an undetermined element of danger in taking Dillinger. It is hoped that he can be taken alive, if possible, and without injury to any agent.

"Yet, gentlemen, this is the opportunity that we have all been waiting for and he must be taken.

"Do not unnecessarily endanger your own lives. If Dillinger offers any resistance, each man will be for himself. It will be up to each of you to do whatever he thinks necessary to protect yourselves in taking Dillinger."

"Boss, why is this twist giving Johnnie up?" Honey asked. "What's in it for her?"

"That's not important," Cowley said.

Purvis shot Cowley a look.

"Anna is getting deported back to the old country," Purvis said. "Romania, I believe. She wants us to intercede with Immigration for her. And she would not mind immunity, either. She operates some houses of prostitution in East Chicago."

"You probably know her, Honey," Hollis said.

"Aw, you just can't trust hookers any more," Honey said. "Your mama is the only one I trust, Hollis."

Cowley's face stiffened. "Now, see here," he said.

"Mormons don't care to hear about hookers," Honey whispered. "Upsets their day."

Purvis's private phone rang. He went into his office to answer it. Seconds later, he popped back out.

"Sage just whispered on the phone," Purvis said. "They're leaving her place in five minutes. Going to either the Marbro or the Biograph. What the hell is the Biograph? I never even heard of the Biograph."

"Don't get wrapped around the axle," Cowley said.

"Biograph?" Purvis said. "Who picked that one? This is turning into Little Bohemia all over again."

"Nervous Purvis," someone whispered near Lee.

"We don't have the men to cover both," Purvis said.

"We don't have the men," Honey said. "We got the lawyers and accountants."

Purvis wiped a bony hand across his face.

"Our plans may change," Purvis said. "They may go to a theater called the Biograph. Sam, all our plans are for the Marbro. We've got maps and everything for the Marbro. Shirley Temple's starring there in Little Miss Marker."

"Inspector," Cowley corrected.

"Inspector Cowley, should we contact the Chicago Police for extra plainclothesmen?" Purvis asked.

"Yes," Cecil said. "If you want Dillinger to escape again."

"I don't figure Johnnie for a Shirley Temple fan," McQueeny said, fanning himself with a newspaper. "And the Marbro is a long walk from Anna Sage's apartment. But the Biograph is just around the corner, on Lincoln Avenue."

"It's good that you know that, Mr. McQueeny," Purvis said.

"How does a San Francisco fella like you know Chicago movie houses so well?" Cowley asked.

"Because that's where he hides out during work hours," Honey whispered. "Watching that clock's hand move for the Government pension."

The bullpen noised up with the agents' nervous talk. One took out his new issue Smith & Wesson .38 and checked the cylinder.

"Holster that," Purvis said. "Check your weapons in the gun vault only. You all know the regulations."

"Listen, gentlemen," Cowley said. "I'm putting you outside in the G-cars. That way, you can get to either theater fast. Phone in here so we can tell you which theater to hit. I'm not authorizing shotguns or Thompsons for this operation. Only sidearms. There's going to be a lot of people on the streets tonight, so the heavy weapons are out. Put a round through a taxpayer, and you will wish that you were that taxpayer. You new men, make sure you have a clear shot before you squeeze one off."

"Don't hit anyone who looks rich enough to sue us," Honey whispered. "If we mess up this one, next month I'll be handing out Ranger rations in West Texas and boring everyone with stories about the Bureau that used to be."

"Naw, Honey," Cecil said. "This is it, the pay-off, the slam-bang big one."

They checked their summer suits to make sure the holsters did not bulge.

"You look a little peakish there," Honey muttered to Lee. Nobody else could hear. "What do you want, what do you say?"

"I want some Bourbon from your flask," Lee said.

"Later," Honey said.

"I want this to be another false alarm," Lee said. "That way nobody has to do anything. Nobody will die. Nobody will criticize. And you and Cecil and I can drink ourselves into trees."

"Sounds good," Honey said. "Safe. Protected."

"All us lawyers wonder the same thing," Lee said. "What are we doing here?"

"Hush up, Lee. We'll talk later."

The agents went downstairs to the new Government Fords, powerful G-cars that had been authorized in the crime bill after Little Bohemia. No one had to use the family car to track gunmen anymore.

Homer Bisbee took the wheel with Lee, Cecil, Honey and Hollis jammed inside the car. They planned to find a pay phone midway between the Biograph and the Marlboro and set up a waiting post there.

"Did you box at Yale, Cecil?" Lee asked.

"I boxed middleweight. I used to do my roadwork across campus with all the little puppies running after me."

"You and your puppies."

The sky over Chicago was tinted orange when the sun went down in the thick heat. Homer Bisbee pulled out from the field office behind four other G-cars.

When they got onto Des Plaines, Homer Bisbee pulled over to the curb.

"We're near the theater?" Lee asked.

"No, I want to stop for a second," Homer Bisbee said. "Pick up a soda pop and some doughnuts."

"Doughnuts," Honey giggled, turning red.

The others hooted at Homer Bisbee. Their jangled nerves relaxed for a minute.

"That's what this job is all about! We should stay in the office waiting for quitting time and having coffee and doughnuts" Cecil patted Homer Bisbee on the rump. "That's Government service for you."

"Doughnuts! Doughnuts!" the others sang out.

Chapter 28: Sunday, July 22, 1934
That Afternoon

CHICAGO, ILLINOIS

Purvis slouched down in the passenger seat outside the Biograph. Winstead was behind the wheel. His forehead sweated under iron-gray hair. The wiry frame eased to the seat cushion, agile for a man of his age. Lee slumped down in the back seat. Everyone had switched cars.

"Mr. Childress," Purvis said. "I'll have to use you as my messenger boy if we see Dillinger. Can you do that?"

"Yessir," Lee said.

Lee wondered how his voice sounded to these two experts. He would shut up in case his voice showed his fear. His shirt cuff showed a wine spot from last night's drinking. The dark summer suit hid a dozen blotches just like it.

They kept their heads back on the seats and looked half asleep. Movement always drew attention to a stakeout.

They scanned the crowd along the sidewalk as people streamed into the theater. Up and down Lincoln Avenue, North Siders milled around in groups. Some were leaning against parked cars, hoping for a breeze off Lake Michigan.

"I already saw this movie," Winstead muttered. "Manhattan Melodrama."

"I bet you're going to tell me what it's about."

"It's a gangster film they lifted out of the New York gambler wars. William Powell plays this honest crusading District Attorney who makes it to the Governor's mansion. Gable is a rocky loveable crook who grew up with Powell. No hypocrite. They were like brothers. Then they went their separate ways. I sure like that Gable."

The Biograph's marquee displayed a banner "Iced For Air" that hung limp in the heat. As darkness settled, the theater's marquee lit up slowly, bulb after bulb.

There were four storefronts between the theater and an alley that connected Lincoln Avenue with Halstead Street. If Dillinger went back to Anna Sage's apartment, he would have to pass by that alley.

"They may not show up at either place," Purvis muttered. "Dillinger has been lucky before. Almost like he can smell a trap."

"There's another team covering the Marbro and that East Chicago copper knows Anna by sight. But we're not using any local cops for firepower?"

"No. The Director wants us to handle this alone. No local assistance."

"Like Little Bohemia."

As time passed, both men scanned the crowds passing by.

"The picture's already started," Winstead said. "They're not coming."

Purvis shook his head. He knew he had to get Dillinger tonight.

"They're not coming," Winstead repeated.

Purvis's mouth opened and shut.

"I think you're right," he said.

Both sat and thought.

Just then, Anna Sage came around the corner with another woman and a man.

The man did not look like Dillinger. He had a heavy moustache and gold-rimmed glasses under his straw hat. Winstead memorized the clothes so he could describe him later: striped white shirt, gray spotted tie, and gray trousers. No jacket.

The younger woman hung on the man's arm. Polly Whosis. Anna walked alongside the couple.

They had come from Fullerton onto Lincoln Avenue. The women waited by the box office while the man bought the tickets. Anna Sage wore a two-piece outfit with a big floppy hat. The marquee lights made her dress look blood red. The man lifted his straw hat as they passed into the theater.

"That's Dillinger?" Winstead asked.

Purvis hesitated.

"It could be Dillinger," Purvis said. "Or it could be Anna's way of cheating us for her own reasons."

"You got to give the word, boss," Winstead drawled.

Lee felt his breath catch up in him.

"What did you say, Winstead?"

"It doesn't look like Dillinger, boss."

"Plastic surgery. That's him, all right. No doubt about it." Purvis took a deep breath and opened the car door. "Mr. Childress, get to a phone and call this in to Cowley. Get everyone else into position."

"Inspector Cowley," Winstead stressed.

Purvis looked up. Lee had never seen Winstead grin before this.

"Cowley's from Washington," Winstead said. "We are your team, boss. Chicago Field Office."

Purvis nodded.

Lee skittered out along the hot sidewalk. The summer suit hung on him.

He saw the men blended into the sidewalk scene. Bloodshot eyes met his. They got the word.

"If this ends here tonight, we can all get some sleep," Cecil said. "Maybe I'll stop screaming at you sometimes, Childress."

"I don't like Purvis alone at the ticket window," Suran said.

"He's got to lead," Cecil said. "You remember the Director's orders. The top-ranking agent on the scene goes in first. That is supposed to make us respect them."

Lee watched Purvis buy his movie ticket and step into the lobby.

Purvis wiped his forehead. He had his service gun and a back-up automatic pinching his belt under the elegant Brooks Brothers jacket.

Purvis looked for the red dress in the lobby and then stepped inside the theater. William Powell was on the silver screen, larger than life. The house was jammed. Chicago was trying to beat the heat.

Purvis unbuttoned his jacket and walked down one aisle and then up another. His ribs heaved.

Now Gable was on the screen. He wore a tuxedo and danced with a blonde starlet at Delmonico's.

Purvis checked the whole orchestra. Nothing. No glint from Dillinger's glasses. The theater was too dark for him to see anything. He went back to the box office. The girl in the box office said the movie had just started and would run 94 minutes.

When Cowley got the call at the field office, he spread the word to the agents phoning in. Then he telephoned Hoover, who was pacing his library in Washington.

After he had talked to the Director, Cowley raced with more agents down to the basement garage. They came roaring up into the Loop, swinging onto the North Side streets, headed for Lincoln Avenue.

All over the city, agents pointed their cars toward the Biograph. Hoover wanted Dillinger taken this time. The street agents wanted the same thing. They were ready to show the Director what they could do.

"Anna Sage kept her word," Purvis said. "Dillinger is with her inside. When Dillinger comes out, I'll light my cigar. That would be the signal to close in."

"You two get along the sidewalk," Purvis said. "Three others in the alley. The rest across Lincoln. If anyone can get to that fire escape, keep that high ground for a better angle of fire. Dillinger may have Baby Face Nelson or some other killer ready to blast us. We won't know until they shoot. We are all in danger here."

Honey walked into the alley with Lee and Hollis. He made sure of his service .38 and loosened his tie.

"Lee, you wouldn't want to quit before we get Johnnie, would you?" Honey said, grinning. "Tell me if you do. Now, no running around once this thing starts. Take a position and keep it."

"Johnnie can't get away."

"Oh, yeah? If Nelson shows up here with a Tommy, you'll see a good arrest plan shot to hell. Nothing ever happens the way it's supposed to on a raid."

Honey was carrying a sawed-off shotgun in his belt. The stock and the barrel were chopped down to eight inches.

"I got some insurance here," he said, showing it.

"That's great," Lee giggled. "We finally got our guns legally and you're still carrying an unauthorized one."

"So is Johnnie."

Winstead stood still in a doorway, watching and remembering gunfights along the Texas Panhandle. He knew the Bureau had hired him for nights like tonight.

Purvis re-checked the film's running time again with the red-haired girl in the box office. She could see Hollis and McQueeny under the marquee, just waiting. McQueeny frightened her. She went back to warn the manager. These characters might be planning a stickup.

The manager scanned the different agents in their business suits. Hollis tried not to notice.

There was no telling how long Dillinger would stay in the theater. He might have spotted the stakeout and would come out dragging a hostage, as he had done on a dozen bank jobs. Or he might have met his buddies inside the theater and they would come blasting their way out any minute now.

The agents chain-smoked and watched the girls go past on Lincoln Avenue.

The manager called the Sheffield Street police station and asked for a Civilian Dress squad. Enough was enough. There were at least a dozen men in business suits hanging around the theater. He asked the squad to check them out.

An unmarked car swung into the alley and hit the agents with its headlights. Honey stayed still and so did Lee. The car rolled up to Hollis and the driver got out with a shotgun in his free hand.

"Federal officers," Honey said quickly.

The copper looked them over, the shotgun leveled.

"Prove it," he said. "Nice and easy, fella."

Honey reached into his inside breast pocket with his left hand. The cop nodded. Honey showed his credentials folder with the small gold badge pinned to the outside.

"We're on assignment after a fugitive," Honey said. "We'll call you if we need you."

"You college boys always need us."

The coppers backed their car through the alley and onto Halstead Street. They swung the car around and drove away.

Inside the theater, Manhattan Melodrama was ending. Gable faced the electric chair bravely. He had taken his chances as a professional crook. Now it was time to cash in his chips.

The curtain came down and the house lights came up.

Dillinger stepped into the aisle followed by Anna and Polly. He looked over the crowd, smiling tightly to himself. He unwrapped a Corona-Belvedere cigar and he stuck it in his mouth. That Clark Gable had style. That was the way to go out.

Outside, two more plainclothes cops stopped Hollis and asked him who he was. Hollis showed his credentials.

"You better tell me what you're doing here," the Civilian Dress cop said. He poked Hollis in the chest. "I got to know."

"Keep your voice down, please," Hollis said.

"This is my city!" the Civilian Dress cop said.

People stopped to gawk.

"Your city is in the middle of my country," Hollis said.

Dillinger walked out of the theater, with a dame on each arm and his cigar lit. If he turned his head to the right, he would see Hollis and the cops.

Then other moviegoers swarmed around him, under the bright lights, blocking his view of Hollis.

The three were now walking near Purvis. Dillinger glanced at Purvis, then looked away.

"Red dress," Honey whispered.

Purvis torched his cigar. It caught. Blue smoke plumed. The agents began closing in. The cops did not move. Hollis stepped to the right, behind Dillinger. Winstead stayed in the doorway. McQueeny, Purvis, and Homer Bisbee drew from under their jackets. Anna let Polly and Dillinger walk on without her. The agents came in closer and separated Dillinger from the crowd.

"Stick 'em up, Johnnie!" Purvis shouted, throwing aside his cigar. "We have you surrounded!"

Dillinger sprinted for the alley, clawing into his pocket. Polly screamed. Winstead and Hollis fired from a combat crouch. Gunfire roared along the avenue. Other agents fired.

Dillinger went down flat and stayed still. Honey held the service gun in both hands. Lee shook alongside him.

Dillinger lay in the alley, his eyeglasses smashed and twisted next to his face, straw hat covering his face.

Purvis ran up shouting. A woman screamed and fell to the ground. Winstead rolled Dillinger's body over. Blood leaked from the eye socket. A blood stain grew on the white-striped shirt. Winstead kicked the Colt automatic away from Dillinger's hands.

"Back!" Hollis came up, moving crabwise through the screaming crowd. "Everyone stay back!"

The streets were filled with agents slowly converging on the fallen gangster.

"Dillinger's dead, boss!" Hollis shouted.

Someone screamed. Lee looked for the hooker Polly. She was lost in the crowd but he caught a glimpse of a red dress. He holstered his gun and moved in Anna's direction but the crowd blocked him. When he looked up, the woman in red was gone.

The crowd surged against McQueeny and Hollis. Purvis looked around, his Colt bobbing in his hand.

"He's dead," Purvis said. "What do we do now?"

"Dillinger has been killed! They got John Dillinger!"

The crowd took up the shout and the agents ran up to form a semi-circle around Dillinger's body and hold them back. Then more agents were moving in a scrimmage line and urging the crowd back onto Lincoln Avenue. The crowd broke and reformed around the body.

"Sam!" Purvis shouted. "Let's go."

Cowley turned towards Purvis, holstering his service piece. He and Purvis jogged back through the crowd to the box office.

"Bureau of Investigation, sweetie," Purvis told the ticket girl, who now looked about thirteen with her face scrunched up and teary.

"I saw it happen," she said.

Purvis lifted the phone and dialed Hoover's library in Washington.

"Yes?" the flat dry voice said on the other end.

"Dillinger's dead, Mister Director," Purvis said. "He resisted."

"I congratulate you and Cowley both," Hoover said. "Fine work."

"Let me talk after you," Cowley said.

Outside, the crowd grew. Kids hooted up and down the alley, running from their parents. They wanted to see the dead bandit. Men dipped their handkerchiefs in the bloodstream along the gutter.

The agents were trying to hold the crowd back.

"Aw, Jesus wept!" Lee said, "These people are crazy!"

"Just bored," Honey answered. "Hard times."

"Who fired?" Cecil asked. "Did either of you?"

"Hell, we'll never know whose shots hit him."

"My money's on Winstead." Honey pointed out the short Texan pacing and chain-smoking near the alleyway.

Honey reached down and shook Dillinger's limp hand.

"So long, Johnnie," Honey said.

Honey faced Lee.

"It doesn't matter who hit him," Honey said. "The Bureau took him down. People are going to respect the Bureau now."

Chapter 29: Monday, July 23, 1934

CHICAGO, ILLINOIS

The next morning, Lee got off the streetcar at Adams Street and walked slowly to the Bankers Building. Chicago felt like a different city to him. The shock still crackled through the city. Some Americans had cried on street corners last night over a Hoosier bank robber.

People talked to each other on street corners, without any introductions.

"Well, they got Johnnie all right," they kept saying.

Everyone felt they had known Dillinger, the way they knew Will Rogers and FDR.

Lee still had work to do. There were three open case files he wanted to close. All three subjects were known: Pretty Boy Floyd, Adam Richetti, and Baby Face Nelson.

His hands still shook when he remembered Little Bohemia. If his nerve held and he could dodge the inspectors, he would hang on a while longer. Honey was right to say he was just a stubborn kid. But he wanted to see those three files closed out.

"Why is Purvis splitting up the office?" Lee asked after lunch.

"He wants to keep control," Suran said. "And he can do this with the younger, new agents coming out from Washington. The rest of us, well, just look around us."

A dozen agents looked each other over mopping up lunch.

"We are a family today," Cecil said. "And Purvis senses that we might group together against him. He is shrewd. Besides, the Director wants us agents transferred so we cannot dispute his version of the Dillinger story. So he grants McQueeny's request for a transfer back to San Francisco. Winstead to Albuquerque and Suran involuntary to New Orleans."

"As an Inspector, Cowley now gets responsible for the entire Midwest."

"I just turned down a pay increase and promotion," Hollis said. "That would have switched me to a desk in Washington."

"You must be screwy," Homer Bisbee said.

"That's what Mr. Purvis seemed to hint," Hollis said. "But I want to stay on the street."

"We'll all get pay increases," McQueeny said.

"I already scored a letter of congratulations," Homer Bisbee said. "For my surveillance of Pretty Boy Floyd's wife and son in their CRIME DOES NOT PAY show. If I accept a transfer to Portland, Maine, I will be promoted to Assistant Night Telephone Supervisor."

"Now there's the path to glory," Cecil said.

"Promotions are the way to go for me," Homer Bisbee said. "A few years and I might become an Inspector's Aide. I can plan surprise inspections of the different field offices and travel cross country."

"I look forward to see you looming over my desk three years from now," McQueeny said. "Heading up that ladder of promotion."

Chapter 30: Saturday, October 20, 1934

EAST LIVERPOOL, OHIO

Earlier that morning, Pretty Boy Floyd had driven out of Buffalo, New York. Adam Richetti was hunched over in the rumble seat, asleep. Their girlfriends, Juanita Baird and her sister Rose, looked out the windows and gossiped about movie stars. Floyd took Route 219 south to Jamestown. They stayed off the big interstates and crossed from the Pennsylvania mountains into Ohio.

Floyd and Richetti had been holed up in a Buffalo flophouse for months, waiting for things to cool off. But the Massacre never cooled off. It was a story that refused to die down. Sunday supplement writers kept milking it on slow days, more than a year later.

They ran photos of Joe Lackey starting to walk again and the morgue shots of Verne Miller.

The radio carried stories about how the feds were cleaning out the Midwest and had shot Johnnie Dillinger in Chi. The feds seemed to be everywhere now. Floyd had decided he should head back to Oklahoma. He was homesick for the hills and planned to hole up there until spring thaw.

They stayed on Route 7, hugging the Ohio River as it flowed south. Floyd figured that he would take a roundabout way and go through Ohio and West Virginia into Kentucky. He wanted to duck the states that had large highway patrols.

Floyd was driving through Ohio fog when the car skidded and slammed into a telephone pole. Nobody got hurt. But the car needed fixing. They stopped a farmer in a Ford truck and asked him to send a mechanic from the nearby town of Wellsville.

They hid in the woods near their car, waiting for the grease monkey. The farmer who owned the land spotted them. He was a tight-fisted Buckeye who did not like hobos on his land. He telephoned the Wellsville constable, Clyde Birch, and told him to run these bums off.

Riding out on horseback, Birch and a volunteer approached the gang. Birch had no gun. He hated the weight on his belt and nothing ever happened in Wellsville. He did not need a gun to chase hobos. Richetti saw Birch's khaki uniform and panicked. He fired a wild shot. The horses took off. Birch and the volunteer hid behind some trees.

The farmer heard the shot. He grouped his hired hands and sons into a posse.

They surrounded Floyd and Richetti, blasting the woods with bird guns. Juanita and Rose surrendered.

Floyd and Richetti ran. Floyd had his pistols and gripped a satchel holding his escape money.

The posse chased Richetti into a ravine. He shot at them and missed. They threw more buckshot at him. Richetti fired without aiming. His gun clicked empty. He was out of ammo.

Two farm hands kicked him around some and slapped him silly with his own empty gun.

The posse tied his wrists with rawhide strips and took him out of the ravine.

Floyd waited longer. His nerves cooled. He flattened out in his business suit with an Army Colt .45 in his hand. The farmers were just rubes with shotguns. He was Pretty Boy Floyd.

One farmer got careless and showed himself.

Floyd shot. The slug hit the farmer's hat.

"I'm dead!" the farmer shouted.

"Not yet," Floyd said.

The hat tore in two. It fell to the dirt.

Floyd saw a large bush move. He fired low into it.

"YEEEOWW!" another rube shouted. "My foot!"

"Cancel your square dance lessons, bub," Floyd said.

Floyd stole away into the woods with his two guns and his bankroll. His fancy two-tone shoes rasped on the grass.

●

Constable Birch brought Richetti into the little Wellsville jail. Dirt showed everywhere on the gray stone floor and the single barred window. It smelled of cigarette smoke and sweat.

"What's your name, tough guy?"

"Get lost and stay there," Richetti said.

Birch slapped him.

"That's just the start," he said. "Shoot at a man without a gun? A man just tryna git along, these times? A working man? Gimme your name, boy."

"Wouldn't tell ya if your pants was on fire."

Birch grabbed Richetti and slammed him head-first into the wall.

"Why you keep falling down? Don't mess up my jail. There any reward money on a bird like you? Don't try lying. I read the Sunday crime story supplements just like everyone else. You might be a Dillinger boy. I'm calling them Chicago G-men collect about you."

Chapter 31: Sunday, October 21, 1934

CHICAGO, ILLINOIS – AKRON AND
EAST LIVERPOOL, OHIO

When the call from Birch came in, Purvis gathered the agents into the bullpen. They all strained to listen to the crackly speaker. The constable described his prisoner.

They realized that the man the constable was holding was Richetti.

And Richetti traveled with Floyd.

"Floyd's hiding out somewhere nearby and these hicks let him get away," Purvis said as he hung up.

Purvis stiffened up. He addressed the assembled agents.

"One squad will set up a temporary headquarters in East Liverpool, near Wellsville," he said. "The other agents will hunt Floyd in the woods. I'll authorize Thompsons and shotguns. No slip-ups, anyone. Let's move out."

●

A few hours later, the chartered plane with the team landed in Akron.

They took rental cars south through the rain to Wellsville.

Lee drove Purvis, Cowley, and Honey along the flat farm roads. They were playing the long shots again. This country seemed too big and there were too many places for one man to hide.

They automatically scanned the faces by the roadside and checked the cars going past. Floyd could be anywhere. They stopped at a diner for coffee and doughnuts. Nobody had seen Floyd around.

Four miles away, Floyd, filthy and rain-soaked in the autumn drizzle, was knocking on the back door of a farmhouse, asking for a meal. The woman who answered figured that he was another hobo in his last dirty suit. They often came to her door from the Illinois Central line that cut through the woods on her property.

She cooked him eggs and potatoes, along with hot biscuits and gravy. Floyd said he needed a ride into Youngstown, just down Route 7. There was a job waiting for him there so he had money to pay for the ride.

The woman said she would see what she could do. When the farm hand came in at noon, Floyd showed him some cash.

"Sir, need a ride into Youngstown," Floyd said. "Cash on the barrelhead. Got it right here."

"Their old truck only runs once in a while," the farm hand said. "Maybe, later on. Right now, I'm hungry. You could ask me again, after lunch."

"Much obliged, sir," Floyd said. "I appreciate you."

The farm hand ate. Floyd paced around the yard, hands in his pants pockets.

●

Birch was holding Richetti in the East Liverpool jail when Purvis and his squad arrived.

Birch opened the door and Purvis strode into the cell.

"Purvis, Bureau of Investigation," he said. "And you're Adam Richetti. You're under arrest for murder. Where's Floyd?"

Richetti wore a torn white shirt one of the cops had given him. His dark hair was combed over a big bald spot. He kept his dark eyes on the floor while Purvis spoke.

Lee was surprised at how young and puny Richetti looked. He had a thin, dark face and a sharp nose like a weasel. It was the face of a cunning sneak thief, not a machine gun murderer.

"Wasn't me," Richetti said. "I wasn't at the Massacre. Your man was wrong. Charley and Vernon went there by themselves."

"When you say 'Charley', you mean Pretty Boy Floyd, right?"

"Sir, I wasn't there. Hope to die if I was."

The constable's telephone clanged.

"Constable's office," Birch said into the phone.

"Yeah, right," the man calling said. "Got a stranger, some city fella, hanging around the Conkle farm on County Road 153. Big fella, fat face."

"Yee-Haw!" Birch said. He slammed down the phone.

"G-men!" he hollered at Purvis in the cell ten feet away. "Reckon we got your fella boxed in!"

Birch and his deputy jammed themselves into the Bureau car. Lee drove. Lee hoped that his own face looked calm. He chewed raw coffee beans to hide his wine breath from last night.

•

When they reached the farmhouse, Lee parked behind a grove of trees for cover. Purvis clenched an unlit cigar in his teeth.

He took a Tommy gun from the trunk and handed it to Lee.

Lee's eyes widened. It was the first time he had carried one on a raid.

Birch and his deputy got behind trees.

"Constable's office!" Birch hollered. "Conkle family, show yourselves !"

Purvis crouched beside the barn.

"Federal officers," Purvis shouted. "Everyone out! You in the house!"

A stooped old man in work clothes appeared at the door. His hands shot up high.

Lee's finger touched the trigger. He stopped in time. His right hand shook.

A woman followed the man, hands clasped over her apron.

"You're looking for that big guy?" She waved her hands like she was shooing the cops away. "He's lit out. It was my boy that phoned Central to call you officers."

The man was still scared.

"Can I put my hands down?" he asked.

"You're lucky to be alive," Purvis said. "That was Pretty Boy Floyd."

"A country fella like him wouldn't hurt plain folks like us," the woman said.

"I've heard that one before," Honey snapped. "Did he say where he was going?"

"Got no idea, sir," the farmer said.

•

The teams split up and scoured the countryside for the next six hours. Purvis was losing his enthusiasm. Honey pushed the men on.

They checked every farmhouse and every barn. Their city clothes were muddy and torn. Their muscles ached from crawling under boundary fences, holding their Thompsons.

They checked one more farmhouse, where the farmer set up coffee for them in the kitchen. The agents slipped into chairs and gratefully drank the coffee, hot and black.

"We missed him," Purvis said. "He's gone. We're wasting valuable time."

This caught the men by surprise and they stirred.

"We've got Richetti," Purvis said. "That's something. We can bring him back to Chicago."

"Mr. Purvis, Floyd is still here," Lee said. "He hasn't gotten away."

"Why do you say that, Childress?" Purvis asked, staring at the agent. "Tell me why you feel that way."

"There's nothing moving on these roads, so he can't walk out of the area without being seen. We've heard that he's only got a handgun, so he can't outshoot a posse.

"And look at his record. He's not that good with a pistol. He always used Tommy guns in all his bank jobs and Kansas City. Sir, we've got him inside a ten-mile area.

"If we stay on him, he'll walk right into us or another squad. He'll have to. But once we pull back, he'll have the whole country to hide in again. I know he's still here and the men agree with me."

Lee knew he was taking a chance by saying this. He had no idea what the men thought.

"Floyd can still be found here, sir," Lee said.

It sounded as though Lee was challenging Purvis. By now, the tiny kitchen had gone too quiet. Purvis looked at the other agents and saw they were hanging on what he said.

"There may be something in what you say, Childress," Purvis said. "I agree with your logic, since you say you've studied the record. And I take it, you'll stand by what you said?"

Lee took a breath.

"Naturally, sir," he said.

The agents rinsed their coffee cups in the sink and piled back into the car.

"What the hell were you talking about Floyd's not being too good with a pistol?" Honey whispered so Purvis could not hear. "Hell, he took out a sheriff who was shooting a Tommy at him. Floyd killed the sheriff with a pistol, face-to-face."

"Well, I had to say something, didn't I?"

"You're learning, Lee. Straight talking doesn't count for any-thing. The only way to make civil servants do po-lice work is to shame and embarrass them into doing it. You shamed Purvis good."

"He said I'd have to stand by what I said, Honey. But how can he hold me responsible if we don't get Floyd?"

"Watch him do it," Honey said.

●

The day stayed gray and drizzly. The sun seemed to set early.

Lee checked his watch when he noticed the daylight was fading. It was just past six. The agents were driving past a farm when they saw a Model T Ford, repainted a light blue, backing down the driveway. Three men sat in the front seat while another man thrashed in the back seat.

"Turn here!" Honey shouted. "Check that car!"

"What do you see?" Hollis asked.

Fifty yards away from the Bureau car, the Ford stopped. Lee swerved the Bureau car around and blocked the road.

Nerves pushed Lee out first. He reached back for his Tommy gun but the stock stuck in the doorway. His left thumbnail sang in pain. Somehow he managed to yank the gun free.

"Federal officers!" Purvis shouted. "Don't move!"

The Model T's doors opened and farmers came out, holding up their hands. A big man in a suit bolted from the back seat and headed into a cornfield.

"He took us prisoner," one of the farmers shouted. "He's got a gun!"

"Floyd!" Purvis shouted. "You can't get away!"

"The hell he can't," Honey said. "Done it before."

Lee touched the Tommy's trigger. The burst drove the gun into his shoulder.

Floyd raised his Colt and shot. The bullet hit Lee's car. Floyd zigzagged through the cornstalks.

The agents fired Tommies and shotguns. The volley hit Floyd. He went down between the corn rows.

The lawmen spread out. They ran across the field.

Floyd lay curled up. Buckshot had taken the belly off him. Honey reached Floyd first and kicked the Colt away. He ran a hand over Floyd that came back blooded.

Lee lowered his Tommy gun. Smoke still spun from the barrel. He coughed so hard that his knees buckled. The gun snout dug in the dirt.

"Talk," Purvis said. He knelt next to Floyd. "You're Pretty Boy Floyd? "

"I'm Charles Arthur Floyd. Who in hell tipped you?" His voice was husky and rough. "Where's Adam? Where's Richetti?"

"Tell us what you know about the Kansas City Massacre."

"Go to hell. I won't tell you sons-of-bitches nothing."

He coughed, lung shot.

"I am Charles Arthur . . . ." Blood bubbled on his lips.

"Tell us what happened, dammit!" Purvis said.

"I am Charles . . . ."

Floyd's head dropped back. His eyes stayed open as his face went slack.

Honey bent down and felt Floyd's pulse in time to feel it quit.

He straightened up and shook his head at Purvis.

"Now we'll never know," Honey said.

Chapter 32: Tuesday, November 27, 1934

BARRINGTON, ILLINOIS

The agents spent weeks running down leads on the remaining gangsters, with no days off.

Two days before Thanksgiving, with a wind that cut their faces, Lee and Cecil were flying down a highway in northern Illinois, looking for Baby Face Nelson. The air outside smelled of wood smoke.

"Some joker calls Purvis," Cecil said. "Wheezes that Baby Face Nelson is supposed to be driving a maroon Ford V-8 with Illinois license plates 639-578. Somewhere near the town of Barrington."

"Why isn't Purvis leading us on this wild goose chase?" Lee asked.

"Some G-men live on a diet of wild goose. He tried to get out with Cowley. But Cowley outranks him and Cowley said no. Cowley took Hollis, our best sharpshooter. Purvis sees himself as America's top gunfighter who brought down Dillinger. Hoover thinks that Purvis believes his own publicity and does not want Purvis in any more newsreels."

"But Purvis didn't even shoot at the Biograph."

"The Director controls that," Cecil said. "He never said who fired. So Ma and Pa Midwest figure that it must be 'Aw-shucks', bashful Purvis, too modest to claim credit. So Cowley's out here somewhere with us. It's a bad idea. Cowley's got guts. But he's a desk jockey, a headquarters man. Not no gunslinger."

"Neither am I," Lee mumbled. "Cowley's just like me."

Cecil did not hear him.

Racing towards Barrington, Lee could see other G-cars searching on the roads behind them. Cecil had scribbled down Nelson's plate number and pinned it to the sun visor.

"An hour ago, I was sitting in a basement on a wiretap, going cuckoo," Lee said. "Thank you, Cowley, for pulling me here."

"He stripped the field office and called everyone at home," Cecil said. "And still we don't have enough agents to track someone like Nelson the right way."

Macadam flew under their wheels. They crested onto Fox River Grove on the Northwest Highway just in time to spot a Ford with Illinois plates, going south. As it sped past, Lee glimpsed the back plate.

"578!" Lee shouted.

Cecil twisted in the seat.

They saw Baby Face Nelson driving the car

Nelson pushed the woman next to him below the dash.

He swung his car around.

"Now he's following us!" Lee shouted.

"He's attacking first," Cecil said. "Just like at Little Bohemia."

Another man poked a long barrel from the back seat. Orange flame bloomed.

"Automatic rifle!" Cecil said.

Cecil yanked his issue piece and cocked it

Nelson drew level with their car. Bullets hit. Lee screamed. Cecil slid down, aimed and triggered three shots. Nelson's windshield shattered. The G-car swerved into the Ford. More slugs hammered the G-car.

"No more!" Lee yelled. His nerves broke wide open. "Pop! Help me!"

Cecil jammed in shells. His lips pulled back over his teeth. He aimed and fired again.

"Lee, sorry that I ride you sometimes," Cecil said.

"Not now!" Lee screeched. "Tell me later! I can't stand this! POP!"

Nelson's car whipped around and fled.

Lee and Cecil were alone on the road.

Their car coughed and bucked.

"Where are they?" Lee howled. "Tell me! Where did they go?"

"They dropped back," Cecil said.

Nelson's car was gone from the flat farm road.

"Let's get a phone and call this is in," Cecil went on. "You scared? Don't be scared, kid. This is the payoff."

Lee saw a turn-off road coming up ahead of them. He yanked the wheel to make the turn. The car skidded onto the shoulder. They bumped over a field, up, down, up, down and stopped dead.

"Our engine's gone!" Cecil shouted. "Nelson killed it."

They jumped out of their car and ran to the road.

Another car flashed past them. Hollis was driving it. Cowley sat next to him. Cowley held a Tommy gun.

"That's Cowley's car!" Cecil shouted.

A few hundred yards away, Nelson's car was still moving fast. Cowley and Hollis roared after him

"Come on!" Cecil shouted.

Cecil and Lee stripped off their topcoats. They ran towards Nelson.

"Cowley's gonna take him!" Cecil shouted. "Hollis is our best shot."

Nelson's car swung around in a U turn. Lee could see the car shake. He dropped to a knee to aim his gun.

"Keep running!" Cecil shouted. "That's too far for a pistol. We need rifles!"

Down the road, Nelson swung over to the side of the road and jammed on the brakes. The car stopped. His engine smoked.

"I got Nelson's car!" Cecil shouted.

Hollis hit his brakes. He just missed Nelson's Ford. Cowley and Hollis saw Nelson's face

"Feds!" Nelson shrieked. "Lousy Feds!"

Far away, a woman jumped out of the car. She ran across the field and lay flat, hands over her head. Nelson's pal put his hands up and froze near their car.

"We got them!" Lee shouted. "Four against one."

Cowley and Hollis scrambled out of their car. They ran for cover. Cowley jumped into the roadside ditch. He loomed big in his topcoat and hat. The ditch did not protect him. It was only three feet deep. Hollis squatted behind the Bureau car.

Baby Face Nelson shot. Hollis fired his shotgun. He hit Nelson with buckshot.

Nelson staggered and started to drop his Tommy gun. He gripped it again. It stayed in his hands.

Cowley fired a burst at him with his Tommy gun. The slugs went low. They tore up the dirt.

Nelson raked the ditch with short bursts.

Lee galloped. His Florsheim shoes slipped. He was still too far to shoot. Something tasting like mud boiled up in his gut. It choked his throat.

Cowley fired his Tommy gun again. Nelson went down and came back up again, yelling.

Lee stopped and took the prone position. He aimed his gun and fired three times. Cecil fired too.

Nelson whipped around. Nelson swung his own Tommy gun. He swept the ditch back and forth, back and forth. Cowley screamed and lay still, topcoat ripped and the hat blown off.

"I'm gonna!" Nelson shouted. "I'm gonna get you!"

Hollis stood up behind the car and hit Nelson with more buckshot. Nelson fired back. Hollis dropped the empty shotgun. Hollis ran to scoop up Cowley's Tommy.

He turned and ran from the car to Cowley's body in the ditch. Nelson fired. Slugs hit Hollis. Hollis flopped down. He touched Cowley's Thompson and lay still.

"Get her and let's get the hell out of here!" Nelson roared.

Nelson staggered to Cowley's car and fell inside.

"Let's take their car!" Nelson shouted. "Grab the guns!"

The woman and Nelson's pal ran to Cowley's car.

Cecil and Lee ran, sixty yards away now.

"Shoot!" Cecil shouted.

Lee and Cecil aimed and fired.

Windows smashed near Nelson.

Lee fired his pistol again.

Nelson's pal cranked Cowley's car. It lurched forward, bumped on rocks, gained the road and skidded.

Lee reloaded with wet hands. He fired again.

The car kept going.

It vanished behind a curve.

●

Lee and Cecil found the Niles Center Hospital and tore through the front doors, coats flapping in the wind.

A nurse pointed them into the tiny emergency room, full of village constables and orderlies.

Cowley was sprawled on a stretcher, gasping, his big head rolled back. The orderlies had slit open his white shirt and cut away the suit pants. Honey burst inside the room, his hair run wild.

Cowley reached out a hand to Lee and snagged his wrist.

"I'm going," Cowley said. "I know I'm going. Did you get Purvis? I must talk to Purvis before I die."

"That's enough, Mr. Cowley," the nurse said as she wheeled him out.

"Inspector," Cowley said.

Lee's shoulders hunched.

"Purvis. I must talk to Purvis," Cowley said as the nurse rolled out of sight.

"You men federals?" The constable looked older than Honey, with a face marked by wind, fists and whiskey. He wore a cracked leather car coat, brass constable's badge turning greenish and canvas clodhopper boots. "We just found a dead fella, up near State Road 63. Blowed to hell and back, slugs and buckshot."

"How big?"

"A runt. No more than five-six. But it's Nelson. Your people got him good."

Lee murmured, "They got him, but he got them."

"Listen, I don't like you G-men," the constable said. "I probably never will. But you college boys, from what I've seen today, you guys . . . ."

He shook his scarred head.

"Sure, pal," Cecil told him, slapping his leather-covered arm. "Sit down and take five. Rest easy. We've been on the same side all along."

Outside the hospital, brakes ripped gravel in the parking lot. Four agents from the Dayton field office hustled through the doorway, looking for Inspector Cowley.

"Here come the rookie agents," Lee said.

"How can you tell they are rookies?" Honey asked.

"Because they look like I used to look, two years ago."

The rookies buzzed outside the operating room. They wanted to see what the dead Baby Face Nelson looked like and to fingerprint him.

Purvis swept inside, wearing his blue Chesterfield coat and smoking a cigar. The cops and nurses recognized him from news photos.

"It's too late, Mr. Purvis," the head nurse said. "Inspector Cowley is already under anesthesia. We had to put him on the table immediately for the operation."

"Yes, of course." Purvis looked numb.

Honey was there, gripping Lee's biceps hard to make contact.

"C'mon, Lee, take a walk. You too, Cecil. My little Yalie."

He walked his friends along the corridor and outside into the chilly fall sunshine. The hospital was surrounded by a wide cornfield that stopped just a few feet from the building.

"I'm scared," Lee said, startling the other two. "I'm still scared, but I've got to do something."

"Lee, you okay?" Honey asked. "You know where you are?"

"Niles Center Hospital, Niles Center, Illinois. Thursday is Thanksgiving. You're Special Agent H.T. Ross." He stopped. His hands were shaking.

Cecil watched and said nothing.

"Honey, I can't do this anymore. This is nuts."

"You know Cowley's going to die," Honey said. "I heard them talking."

"We're going to nail Nelson's pal somehow," Lee said. "At some crossroads at three AM. We're going to shotgun him and Nelson's whore and all the others."

"Sure we will." Honey was talking low, trying to calm him down. "We can do it easily now, Lee. We got what we need now. So does the country. We got the power, the Tommies and the funding."

"Straighten up," Honey whispered. "In a little while, you'll have to report to the Director on the phone what happened here."

Icy air blew on Lee.

"Feel that wind coming down?" Lee said. "My own flat land. Roads going on for miles and miles. Jobless people walking them now. Just to have something to do. I wonder how I will feel, walking them. If it wasn't for the Bureau, I would be walking along Shad Road tonight to fish."

They watched the wind whip the trees.

"I'll tell the Director the truth, Honey," Lee said. "I've got to leave the Bureau. I don't want to but I have to. Ask Cecil about the gunfight today. If I stay in, I'll get someone killed. This just isn't for me."

"What are you talking about?" Cecil asked.

"I've been feeling this way since the first shootout," Lee tried to smile. He faced them. "Now that I've made up my mind, it's a relief to say it out loud."

Lee could see them both shake their heads

"You're full of surprises, kid," Honey said.

"Seeing Nelson kill winds me all up," Lee said. "Like usual, I'll need some Dago red to sleep okay tonight. But this is my last gunfight, ever."

"Take the night off," Cecil said. "Stop thinking so much."

"In this Depression, any job is a good job," Lee said. "But now the Depression is starting to end. I belong in a law office somewhere while the hard times finally turn better. I don't belong here and that's why I'm going to quit."

"You should have said something," Cecil said. "We all threaten to quit. Some do it every day. But this is just too quick. We can talk it over."

Lee shook his head. The icy sunlight caught his silver spectacles.

"Let's go into Niles Center," Honey said. "There's the Blind Pig shot-house bar, home cooking, where we can eat and relax."

"Not any more, Honey," Lee said. "You see that fashion-plate bureaucrat Melvin Purvis over there?"

Purvis was standing just inside the hospital doors, with his back to them

"I know what I have to do now," Lee said. "It is all in our Manual. Go over there, surrender my issue weapon and credentials and badge to the Special-Agent-in-Charge and resign."

Lee started and then stopped.

"Whatever you decide," Honey said "we're both proud of you. You have served. Now you can go back to lawyering. Find a wife, have kids, thicker glasses, rest and fat up. Now you can be like everyone else."

Lee nodded, swallowing. He pushed open the glass doors and walked over to Purvis, reaching inside his breast pocket for the leather credentials case.

SPECIAL THANKS ONCE AGAIN TO…

To Detective-Investigators Mark Baldessare and Gerry Mc-Queen and all the other cops and federal agents who taught me so much about hunting our real-life serial killers.

To Gabriel Geoffroy for his eagle-eyed proofing.

To the ever patient Dave Bass for book design.

To Nad Wolinska for her always inventive cover illustrations.

To Richard Amari for his equally inventive cover design.

To my screenwriting partner, Lynwood Shiva Sawyer, for his support and encouragement over the years.

To the *Spy, the Movie* team – Jim MacPherson, Alex Klymko, Charles Messina and all the rest of the gang for a grand adventure in screenwriting.

If you enjoyed reading ***Real Cops***, you'll definitely like Frank Hickey's Dancing Max Royster Mystery Series

•

Dancing Max Hits Guadalcanal
or
When In Doubt, Rhumba

I, Dancing Max Royster, sixty-five, paunchy, jovial and carefree, teach ballroom dance during the Manhattan winter.

Diana, my lover from twenty-three years ago, comes to me to inform me that terrorists in the South Pacific island of Guadalcanal have kidnapped her daughter, Rua.

She also whispers to me that I am Rua's father.

She begs me to rescue OUR daughter.

At my age and girth, hating guns and violence, I cannot act like a tough young jungle fighter.

But I must try.

In Guadalcanal, I witness gunfights and terrorist bombings. Melanesian locals fight each other over immigration.

A charming radical named Ugi stirs up his followers as he outwits the unarmed local police. To blend in and gather data, I teach ballroom dance.

During a tango, I hear that Rua had gone to Marau Island, far off the coast. Only one boat goes there, captained by the profane Pakistani, Gul. He worships the late American singer, Laura Nyro, and has named his boat in her memory. Somehow, I talk my way onto his boat.

As we embark through the crocodile infested waters, Ugi's terrorists swarm over the good ship Laura Nyro. We fight back with antique guns and fists and at last drive them from the vessel.

When we reach Marau, we discover that Ugi has kidnapped Rua and will kill her unless I act. Aided by a beautiful island woman and a somewhat unreliable Tommy gun, I prepare for the final battle to free Rua.

Love Finds Max at Christmas
or
Kissing in the Slush After Sixty

Frosty Manhattan Christmas. Our hero, Max waltzes with Peg, the mysterious beauty. A White cop kills an unarmed Black man and the city explodes in a night that goes on forever

The city throws a Unity Holiday Party, a dancing street fair to bring all together.

I, Max, 62, meet and flirt with a dark blonde beauty named Peg, a barmaid with no illusions left. Her looks and slangy streetwise talk hold me. At my age, she makes me smolder and feel 24 again.

No matter what it takes, I want her for mine.

But the plan smashes when a drunken Black man fights with a White rookie cop. The Black man dies and everyone hollers their own ideas about what really happened.

Seeing a chance to hit big on a settlement, I summon Nancy, a hooligan street-fighter with a lawyer's ticket. This kind of death means cash.

Peg is the only witness to the struggle between the drunken man and the cop. If I can run this, I can stop hustling forever.

Skip, another lawyer, Black, my nemesis-father figure, always scheming, hijacks Peg for his reward. His bodyguard, Joey, beats me in a fight.

The FBI and the radical group SAP-Stop Aggressive Police-jump into this case. Trying to out-dance them, I go undercover in SAP and live like a radical.

Through freezing stakeout nights and bitter dawns, I must find Peg and love at Christmas.

Max Wisecracks Hollywood
or
Foxtrotting for Justice

I, Max Royster, cannot run fifty yards or see my own feet under a beer belly.

Pushing sixty-four years old, I struggle to rebuild, after the New York cops fired me for depression and hijacked my pension.

Like everything else sliding around loose, I wind up in Hollywood, California.

By chance, I see a female Black LAPD cop grapple with a homeless woman, an ex-Blaxploitation film actress who 40 years ago turned Civil Rights radical.

The homeless woman dies.

Sidewalk Angelenos heave rocks and bottles in protest.

Los Angeles screams. Cops retreat and haul me to the station.

An ambitious Deputy District Attorney and the hard-charging FBI play witness tug-of-war over my fast-aging body. Everyone wants to jail me as a material witness for trial.

To stay clear, I go underground with a cryptic Hollywood beauty and learn much on the floor of her apartment. The media turns up the heat. The G-men freeze my cash.

All that I have left are my wits and the cash in my blue jeans.

When the Whistle Blows, Everyone Goes

Federal agents jail me for murder. That's me, Max Royster. Aging. Fat. Broke. And innocent. How do I clear myself from inside my cell? Nobody believes me. A hate group tries to rape and kill me. But Mother Royster always said to keep smiling no matter what. So to chase away the jailhouse blues, I organize a hipster group and swing dances among the inmates.

A Manhattan tycoon frets about his beautiful daughter.

She is cavorting somewhere near Palm Springs, California.

He pays me, Max Royster, to find her.

This simple job turns into a hairball.

She leads me astray.

Someone kills her boyfriend.

The U.S. Park Rangers blame me for it and lock me up in a federal prison.

Me being me, I try to stay cheery by organizing swing dances between male inmates.

An inmate hate group tries to rape and kill me.

Other inmates protect me for kicks.

Some enjoy the dances. Anything beats prison routine.

The warden and the correction officers suspect me of spying on them for the FBI.

Things look grim for our hero.

Can I swing-dance and laugh my way out of lock-down to find the real killer among the Beautiful People in Palm Springs?

Everyone wants to see what happens next.

You will, too.

Softening Flatbush

I, Max Royster, fat, broke, divorced, thrown off the NYPD for mental illness. Now in Flatbush, Brooklyn, I find new love, new murder and new career. Can I keep my love? Crack the case? Can I inspire and change private security? And maybe regain my NYPD shield?

Flatbush, Brooklyn, a neighborhood that used to be the borough's jewel.

Sixty years later, street crime plagues the area.

My love, Cooper, and her friends want to clean up the neighborhood and improve Flatbush's image. That way, they can 'flip' their homes and triple their profits

I join a security agency, thinking I can transform the guards from unhappy minimum wage-earners to passionate, hardworking crime fighters.

If I succeed and make Flatbush safe for Cooper and her friends, we will buy a home there and enjoy a happy marriage.

My new employees and I fight to take back the Flatbush streets. I give them better training, uniforms and weapons. The guards buff their new badges with pride.

My boyhood friends, out-of-work actresses, barflies and story-tellers, join us in our quest.

But some guards refuse to let go of old vices. Others turn vigilante and bully innocents.

Curbing their zeal, I try to teach them to uphold civil rights as I hunt the suspect in the comedian's murder.

Then, under cover of night, good and evil clash at the Lefferts Historic House. Facing disgrace and prison, I must decide what matters most in life to me.

Come walk with me on that razor edge between brutality and staying alive as Cooper and I, my Flippers and my guards give everything to try *Softening Flatbush.*

Can Showbizzers Crush Crime?

Can I, Max Royster, fired from the NYPD for mental disease, on crutches, train a ragtag group of performers, my Showbizzers, to use their skills and bodies to stop a genius crime lord in the High Desert town of Basta, California?

Freezing, grieving my lost shield, I hobble aboard an Amtrak train. America passes by outside my window.

When we reach the California desert, my spirits rise. Hope for a new life makes me exit in the small sandy town of Basta.

The sun and beauty cheer me. But the town suffers from crime. A thug mugs me, taking my cash and ID.

That turns me sad again.

A group that I dub "My Showbizzers" – out-of-work dancers, actresses, dog trainers and writers – rescue me. They remind me of my live-for-the-moment cronies back in Manhattan, "The Playpen Irregulars." Thrilled by their energy, I fall in love with Koy, a beautiful Asian dog-handler.

Some Basta deputies duck work or bully innocents. Their sloppiness angers and frustrates me, and their laziness helps a local criminal genius, Crostwaite, rob a bank.

My Showbizzers have many skills. Maybe they could use those talents and creativity to fight crime. They might do better than some lazy deputies.

Nobody else believes in my idea. Locals mock me. The sheriff and the FBI block me. But I force myself to push my idea forward, while my Showbizzers must fight their own bias against government and rules.

But when Crostwaite starts killing, I train my Showbizzers. They go undercover. Their beautiful bodies use sex as a weapon.

To avenge his childhood of horrors, Crostwaite vows to destroy Basta.

Frightened but passionate, without guns, power or respect, my Showbizzers and I risk everything to stop Crostwaite.

Our deadly showdown will answer the question once and for all: ***Can Showbizzers Crush Crime?***

Brownstone Kidnap Crackup

When Max witnesses a debutante's kidnapping, he becomes the FBI's prime suspect. Or is he actually their salvation?

It's Christmas in Manhattan.

A blizzard whips the city.

The Beautiful People, in the elite Upper East Side, celebrate in their brownstones.

Until a kidnapper seizes a beautiful young debutante.

Max Royster, fired from the NYPD for mental illness, fights the kidnapper but loses.

The kidnapper flees. Stripped of gun, shield and power, Max has only his wits to save the victim.

The FBI treats Max like a suspect and tramples roughshod on his rights.

During this long sleepless night, an unknown FBI agent cracks up. Over the radio, he quotes J. Edgar Hoover and plants false clues.

To solve the case, Max must smash through the facade and mysteries of millionaires in their snug brownstones.

Exotic women tempt him to give up.

The blizzard worsens.

As the winds howl and snowdrifts deepen, Max risks his life and his freedom in a desperate bid to save the victim.

Once again, Max Royster is back on the street in ***Brownstone Kidnap Crackup.***

Funny Bunny Hunts the Horn Bug

To catch a sex killer targeting Upper East Side beauties, misfit NYPD cop Max Royster goes undercover…as an NYPD cop!

The Upper East Side of Manhattan is one of the richest neighborhoods in the world.

Max Royster, a maverick, outspoken and erudite NYPD foot patrolman, has been nicknamed "Funny Bunny" by his fellow cops.

Late one night, patrolling wealthy brownstones, he sees a burglar attacking a rich actress. Max chases him. They fight but the burglar escapes.

The burglar is a sexual predator, known in cop-speak as a "Horn Bug".

For losing the suspect, Max's captain deems Max "a Funny Bunny," too unstable for police work. He strips Max of his gun and badge, then orders Max into Bellevue Hospital for observation and maybe for the rest of his life.

Without any tools or support, Max has ten days as to stop this Horn Bug from killing again.

The Gypsy Twist

Max Royster's hunt for a sadistic serial killer takes a startling turn when he realizes that not all predators are born alike.

One autumn night, someone strangles a teenage boy jogging in Central Park.

In Brooklyn, street cop Max Royster risks his life to disarm a madwoman with a knife without harming her. Nevertheless, her lawyer charges Max with brutality. The Department decides to punish Max.

Max's protector is Sgt. Lipkin, an expert detective working the Central Park murder. Lipkin knows that a killer like this seeks a new sexual thrill, a "Gypsy Twist," with each new murder. The dead boy is the son of one of the wealthy elite of the Upper East Side.

Lipkin summons Max for the assistance that only Max can provide.

Max probes the tony school and neighborhood, ignoring bosses who, out of jealousy, try to block his progress.

A beautiful, free-spirited reporter, Diana, woos Max to try and make him reveal insights about the case. Denying him nothing, she lures Max onward.

The killer seizes another school-boy who was playing soccer in the park and drags him to death with a car.

Wealthy New Yorkers scream that someone is butchering their sons. The city rocks.

One night, muggers attack Sgt. Lipkin and Max, who freezes on the trigger. The muggers cripple Lipkin.

The Department moves to fire Max.

But the dead boy's tycoon father hires Max to track down the killer. Max and Diana live below the radar in the New Orleans and San Francisco underworlds, hunting the killer until a shocking conclusion reveals the killer's true identity.

www.ingramcontent.com/pod-product-compliance
Lightning Source LLC
Chambersburg PA
CBHW071409100726
47908CB00004B/1112